Fernwood

Fernwood

MARCELLA THUM

PUBLISHED FOR THE CRIME CLUB BY

DOUBLEDAY & COMPANY, INC.

GARDEN CITY, NEW YORK

1973

*All of the characters in this book
are fictitious, and any resemblance
to actual persons, living or dead,
is purely coincidental.*

First Edition

ISBN: 0-385-05310-x
Library of Congress Catalog Card Number 73–81416
Copyright © 1973 by Marcella Thum
All Rights Reserved
Printed in the United States of America

Fernwood

CHAPTER ONE

It was late on a muggy August afternoon, the sky dark gray and swollen overhead, when I returned to my boardinghouse and found my landlady poised, waiting for me in the dimly lit front hall. My first thought was the back rent I owed. Lately Mrs. Carson had been dropping discreet but pointed hints . . . "I hate to bother you, my dear . . . so distressing under the circumstances . . . still it has been two months."

Well, I no longer had to make embarrassed excuses, at least not for a while, I thought. My hand involuntarily reached up to touch my high-boned collar, around which, until an hour ago, my mother's pearl necklace had hung.

Before I could speak, however, Mrs. Carson almost jerked me into the hallway. Her voice rose, agitated. "My dear, I'm so relieved you're back. If you'd only told me . . . he's been waiting for you in the parlor for half an hour now . . . I had no idea you were acquainted with Jason Barclay."

"I'm not," I blurted, startled by the look of awed respect and something else, a greedy curiosity in my landlady's usually placid face.

"But Mr. Barclay particularly asked for you by name. Naturally I assumed you knew him or I would never have . . ." She broke off, casting a worried glance toward the velvet portiered parlor, and lowered her voice to a whisper. "Perhaps your dear father . . ."

I shook my head. Father and I had known no one in the city of Richmond when we came South for his health six months before. My father's illness, his increasing debilitating condition, had made it impossible for us to make any friends. Not, I thought wryly, that two transplanted New Englanders could find friends easily in a city that after almost thirty years still clung to its painful memories of the Civil War that had ravaged the South.

"No, I'm sure if father knew anyone in Virginia he would have told me." My throat constricted, remembering only too well that part of the agony of my father's last days was caused by the knowledge that he was leaving me, not only practically penniless, but alone in a strange city without family or friends.

"Then why . . . I don't understand." Mrs. Carson's white hands fluttered mothlike to her pink, plump face; her round eyes, shocked. "If you've never been properly introduced, why should Mr. Barclay call upon you?"

"Suppose I ask him and find out," I replied briskly.

Pausing at the hall mirror, I withdrew the long pins that anchored my feathered hat, carefully removed it and absently smoothed the dark wings of hair beneath. It had been a long time, I suddenly realized, since I had looked, really looked, at myself in a mirror. And for a moment I hardly recognized the young woman staring back at me. A pale triangle of a face with hardly enough flesh to cover the unusually high cheekbones, shadows like ink smudges beneath the dark eyes, lines of strain pulling at the corners of an overly generous mouth. I shrugged mentally. Well, I had never been a raving beauty to begin with. Aunt Agnes had always deplored what she called "my odd, foreign" looks. Certainly I was much too tall and full-bodied for the willowy Gibson Girl figure that was all the vogue these days.

Turning away from the mirror, I walked quickly into the front parlor. The lamps in the parlor were turned down low, too. Mrs. Carson didn't believe in wasting kerosene. At first, all I was aware of was my visitor's size, a great bear of a man whose shadow seemed to engulf me as well as the small room. Then, as I turned up the table lamp and the pool of yellow-orange light lapped outwards, I could distinguish his face. Unruly rust colored hair and heavy, homely features that had been chiseled haphazardly. One eyebrow was set sardonically higher than the other, the broad-bridged nose slightly off center, a full-lipped mouth surprisingly sensual above a no-nonsense squared chin.

The skin of the face had the terra-cotta, weathered appearance of a sea captain or a farmer. White lines splayed out from the eyes as if they were narrowed often against the sun. The eyes themselves, however, had borrowed no warmth from the sun. They were the chill, washed blue of a January sky.

Then I became aware that as intently as I was scrutinizing my visitor, he was studying me. It had been a long time since any man had gazed at me in such an appraising fashion. I felt a flush climb my cheeks. "Mr. Barclay? I'm Abigail Prentice. You wished to see me?"

He took a step toward me and his heavy stride made the fragile porcelain figures on Mrs. Carson's whatnot shelf tremble. His voice was deep and brusque. "You're younger than I expected."

"I'm twenty-five," I bristled. "And I don't see what business . . ." I broke off, all at once seeing the copy of the Richmond *Ledger* he held in one large hand. "Oh, of course, I'm sorry. You've come in answer to my advertisement. Please sit down."

He glanced around, located a chair that looked as if it might bear his weight and dropped into it gingerly. Then, as if remembering his manners, apologized gruffly. "Forgive me for not writing first, Miss Prentice, but I only saw your advertisement today and I'm leaving for Fernwood in the morning so there isn't much time." He scowled at me unhappily. "Frankly, I expected a schoolteacher to be a somewhat older woman."

I sat down across from him, folding my hands in my lap to hide their trembling. "My qualifications are exactly as stated in my advertisement, Mr. Barclay. I graduated from Vassar College in 1888 and taught school for four years before my . . . my father became ill and decided to come South for his health." I hesitated for a moment then added, "He died two months ago."

Did I imagine, I wondered, the touch of compassion that for a moment warmed those icy blue eyes. Then he inclined his head gravely. "Again my apologies, Miss Prentice, for intruding upon your grief. I assume then you're not from Virginia?"

"My home is . . . was in Worcester, Massachusetts."

He lifted a puzzled eyebrow. "You're not planning to return North? Surely, you have friends, family concerned about you."

"I have an aunt in Boston," I said, not adding that I doubted if Aunt Agnes was particularly concerned about me, especially since she hadn't even bothered to reply when I wrote her of her brother's death. "Otherwise there was just my father and myself."

A smile for a moment flickered across the broad face, softening the craggy features, and I lowered my estimate of the visitor's age. Not as old as I had first thought, I decided, somewhere in his mid-thirties, perhaps. "Forgive me again, Miss Prentice, I don't mean to pry. It's only that our Southern families are seldom so . . . so limited in size." The smile faded, the frown returning. "In any case, after your loss, it's natural to suppose that a young woman alone would want to return to her own country."

"It was my impression that Virginia and Massachusetts were in the same country," I replied. And immediately regretted my tartness. I must learn to guard my tongue, I thought exasperated. Even though my father had always encouraged and expected me to speak my mind, to use my intelligence to the fullest extent, most men, I had already discovered, resented outspokenness in women. And heaven knows, I needed this job. It was foolish to take the chance of antagonizing Mr. Barclay.

I softened my voice and attempted to change the subject. "You haven't yet told me about the position, Mr. Barclay. Would I be teaching in a school?"

"You'd be employed as a tutor for a young boy."

So he was married, I thought, and felt an odd stab of disappointment. "How old is your son?"

"It's not my son," he said curtly. "It's my nephew. He's eight and, I might add, not a very apt pupil. It would be best, of course, if he could attend school with other students his age but there is no decent private school near Fernwood. And his aunt, who lives at Fernwood and raised the boy after my brother's death, refuses to send Quentin away to boardingschool. She feels he's too frail."

I couldn't help catching the note of dislike . . . no, not that strong, I decided, distaste in the man's voice when he spoke of his nephew. And without even knowing the boy, felt a stirring of sympathy for him.

Mr. Barclay shrugged impatiently. "The truth is my sister-in-law has spoiled the boy rotten. The last tutor we had stayed only three months, the one before that, four weeks."

"I'd stay," I blurted, and bit my lower lip to stop its trembling. The pearl necklace I had pawned had brought me only enough money to pay my back rent and buy a train ticket North. Once I reached Worcester, I would again be penniless. And that would mean throwing myself on the not very tender mercies of my Aunt Agnes. Oh, she would allow me to live with her, of course, in her museum-like mansion on Beacon Hill, but grudgingly, never letting me forget I was living on her charity. She had never forgiven her brother for becoming a professor, instead of entering into her husband's textile business, or for marrying a foreigner, instead of the proper Boston girl she had picked out for him.

Carefully now I forced myself to relax, to smile with what I hoped was confidence. It would never do for Mr. Barclay to guess how desperate I was for the position. "I've taught classrooms of forty pupils. One small boy shouldn't be much of a problem for me."

Mr. Barclay gazed at me thoughtfully. "We live a very quiet country life at Fernwood. The plantation isn't close to any town, or any other plantation for that matter. There is very little social life or entertainment. I'm afraid a young woman like yourself would find it dull."

My heart beat more quickly. It sounded as if he were seriously considering me for the position. "I'm accustomed to living quietly," I said. "And I don't require . . . entertainment."

"We couldn't pay a great deal," Mr. Barclay continued bluntly, naming a monthly sum. It was less than I had hoped for but apparently food and lodging would be included. If I were frugal, within a year, I should be able to save enough to return to Worcester and support myself until I could find another teaching job, without the humiliation of turning to my aunt for assistance.

Mr. Barclay got to his feet. I had the feeling that he was a man who made up his mind quickly and his indecision now about me was aggravating to him. Or was it only that he wasn't used to dealing with young ladies, I wondered. Would that explain the curious awkwardness of his manner, the stiff way he held himself, as he said, "Perhaps you should think about it overnight, Miss Prentice, before you make a decision. I can stop by in the morning . . ."

I couldn't take that chance. How did I know but once he left, he would reconsider, decide I was too young or too inexperienced. It was obvious he was only half convinced. I got to my feet, too. "Please, Mr. Barclay, I assure you there's no need for delay. I can quite easily leave with you in the morning."

I heard the urgency creep into my voice, but I couldn't help myself. Jason Barclay's was the one and only answer I had received to my advertisement that I had placed so hopefully in the *Ledger* two weeks before.

I felt that icy blue gaze probing, searching my face and was sure he saw the desperation in my eyes, even noticed the carefully mended white jabot at my neck, the frayed cuffs on the mutton sleeves of my dress. And was suddenly furious with myself for having exposed myself to that cold, impersonal survey.

"There is something else," he said finally, reluctantly, as if coming to a decision. "My sister-in-law, like many other Southerners, lost a great deal in the war. Her family home here in Richmond was burned to the ground, her father shot to death before her eyes. Her husband, my brother Guy, came back from a Northern prison camp with his left arm gone. She has little affection for Yankees, I'm afraid."

I tried in vain to read that remote, impersonal gaze. Then couldn't resist asking, "How do you feel about . . . Yankees?"

He shrugged, his voice carefully indifferent. "The South gambled and lost. I'm not a great believer in lost causes. Anyway, the Barclays were more fortunate than most. At least, we were able to hold on to our land. We didn't lose Fernwood. That's all that matters."

When he spoke of the plantation, for the first time a warmth touched his eyes like sunlight moving in the depths of a deep, quiet pool. The harsh lines of his face softened, relaxed. I wondered suddenly if any woman had been able to put that look on Jason Barclay's face.

Then, embarrassed at what I was thinking, I hastily held out my hand. "Thank you for accepting me, Mr. Barclay. I'll do my best not to disappoint you."

For a moment he looked startled, as if he weren't aware he *had* accepted me for the position, then he shrugged, a look of amused respect touching his eyes as he took my hand. My own hand seemed to disappear into his large one. His skin felt rough against mine, work-hardened, but what momentarily shocked me was the unexpected warmth from his flesh tracing a path up my arm, racing like fire through my body. For a moment my whole body felt strangely warmed, as if I had been cold for a long time and hadn't realized it.

Still holding my hand, he frowned down at me. "Perhaps you shouldn't thank me yet, Miss Prentice. I'm not sure I'm doing you any favor. If you should have second thoughts, you can reach me at the Palace Hotel. Otherwise, we'll leave from the hotel at ten o'clock in the morning."

I withdrew my hand, smiling confidently. Later, remembering that moment, I would wince at the complacency in my voice as I replied smugly, "You'll find that I'm not in the habit of changing my mind, Mr. Barclay. I'll be at the hotel at ten in the morning."

CHAPTER TWO

A few minutes after Mr. Barclay left and I had returned to my room on the third floor, a knock came at my door. My landlady stood on the threshold, a frosty pitcher and two glasses on a tray in her hands. "Such a hot day," she panted, her face flushed from the exertion of the climb up the narrow staircase. "I thought you might like a cool drink."

"Thank you, that would be nice." I stepped back, smiling gratefully, though I suspected it was curiosity, not lemonade, that had driven my landlady up the steep flight of stairs. "As a matter of fact, I was about to look for you. I want to settle my bill. I'll be leaving in the morning."

"You're returning North?"

"No." I hesitated then decided there was no reason why Mrs. Carson shouldn't know. "I've accepted a position as tutor for Mr. Jason Barclay's nephew."

"Fernwood? You're going there?"

Mrs. Carson set the tray down so abruptly the glasses clattered.

"I believe that's the name of the plantation. Why? Do you know it?"

Mrs. Carson became very busy, pouring lemonade, her back to me. Her voice was flustered. "Oh, my, yes. Fernwood was only twenty miles from our own plantation of Glenview. Of course, Fernwood was much larger, over two thousand acres of prime tobacco land and more than three hundred slaves. And Fernwood Hall . . ."

She turned and handed me a glass of lemonade, her faded eyes glowing. "I remember attending a ball there a few months after the start of the war. The ballroom was filled with ropes of smilax and pink and white damask roses from Fernwood's gardens. Charlotte Barclay—she was Charlotte Ramsay then—had had her gown especially made in Paris to match the color of the roses. She was already sweet on Guy Barclay at the time even though he was only seventeen. Later, when they married, there were some who thought Guy had married beneath himself. The Ramsays were in business, you know, in Richmond, had been here only a few generations, while the Barclays, naturally, are one of the oldest families in Virginia. Still, it was Ramsay money that kept the Barclays going after the war when so many other plantations went under."

A bitterness shadowed the plump face. My landlady, I was sure, was remembering her own lost plantation of Glenview. There were many other elderly widows like Mrs. Carson I had met in Richmond, husbands killed in the war, homes destroyed or lost to ruinous taxes, women forced to eke out a precarious existence, running boardinghouses, taking in genteel sewing when once they had been mistresses of wealthy plantations with dozens of servants to do their bidding.

Thoughtfully I sipped at my glass of lemonade. It occurred to me that since I soon would be working at Fernwood, it might be helpful to find out as much as I could about my future employers. And I had already discovered there was nothing my landlady loved more than a good gossip.

"Are the Barclays a large family?" I asked.

Mrs. Carson settled herself comfortably in a chair and reached for her palmetto fan. "Let me see . . . William and Martha Barclay had four sons as I recall. Guy, the oldest, joined the Army when he turned eighteen, two weeks after his marriage to Charlotte. He was badly wounded at Pittsburg Landing and taken prisoner. His father was a colonel on Lee's staff and made it through the war without a scratch and then tragically was killed in the last month of the war in some minor skirmish. Mrs. Barclay was carrying their youngest son, Rob, when the news reached her of the colonel's death. The shock brought on an early birth. The child survived but the mother unhappily died." Mrs. Carson sighed and waved the palmetto fan gently. "Poor

Martha. She was a Curtis, you know, related through marriage
to the Byrd family . . ."

"You said there were four sons," I prodded quickly before she
got too involved in her favorite sport of climbing family trees.

"Oh, yes." The fan moved faster. "Well, of course, there's
Jason and his twin brother Brian. They were only babies when
the war began. I hardly knew them."

I tried to imagine a duplicate of the man I had met in the parlor and could not. "Twins?" I asked, startled.

"Not identical twins, not at all," Mrs. Carson said hastily.
"Even as children the difference was very marked."

"Then there are several brothers still living at Fernwood."

Mrs. Carson shook her head. "Unhappily the Barclays have
had more than their share of misfortune. Guy was thrown from
his horse and killed several years back. Rob, the youngest boy,
is supposedly studying for the law here in Richmond but from
what I hear spends most of his time at the gaming tables." Mrs.
Carson made a prim mouth of disapproval. "Rob, I'm sorry to
say, takes after his older brother Brian."

"Brian Barclay . . . does he live at Fernwood?"

Mrs. Carson hesitated a moment then said slowly, "No, he
left Virginia some years ago and made, I hear, an unfortunate
marriage in New Orleans. He had already lost all of his inheritance through gambling and drinking. When he and his wife
died in a cholera epidemic, their son, Quentin, just a baby, was
sent back to Fernwood to live. It's Quentin who will be your pupil. Charlotte Barclay raised him and I understand simply dotes
on the boy. But then she and her husband never had any children of their own."

"Have you ever met the boy?" I asked curiously.

"Once, about a year ago, I ran into Charlotte with Quentin,
shopping here in Richmond. A very ordinary little boy, he
seemed to me, towheaded, and I don't doubt with a streak of
temper like all the Barclay men. I must confess I was surprised
to see Charlotte at all. They say she seldom budges from Fernwood these days, nor Jason either for that matter. Of course, in

Mr. Barclay's case, it's understandable, after what happened . . ."

Mrs. Carson's voice trailed away. Her eyes rested on me warily and I had the feeling that all of my landlady's seemingly rambling conversation, had been leading up to this moment, to this particular revelation. And although I had been anxious to learn all I could about the Barclays, suddenly I found I didn't want to hear any more. Yet, having deliberately opened Pandora's box, I knew it was useless to try and close it again.

"Happened?" My voice sounded brittle.

Mrs. Carson delicately patted the perspiration on her lips and brow with a lacy handkerchief before she once again picked up the palmetto fan and the thread of her conversation. "Well, of course, it was all a long time ago. Jason took the grand tour of Europe in 1884. He was always more interested in books and art, that sort of thing, than the other Barclay men. In Paris he met and fell in love with a beautiful French girl, Celia Rougier. He brought her back to Fernwood. All the wedding plans were made. Then the night before the wedding, there was a terrible accident. The girl shot herself."

"Shot herself!" Despite the tinder box heat in the bedroom, I shivered as if a chill draft had suddenly drifted in from the still dusk, gathering outside the window. "How? Why?"

"No one knows exactly. She was alone in her bedroom at the time, apparently examining a set of dueling pistols that belonged to Brian Barclay. I don't suppose she knew anything about guns. She was raised in a French convent. One of the guns accidentally went off . . ." Mrs. Carson shrugged unhappily. "Jason took her death very hard. I never met the girl myself but I understand she was extraordinarily beautiful. I don't think Mr. Barclay ever got over her death. And then, unfortunately, there was all the gossip . . ."

"What sort of gossip?" I asked uneasily.

For the first time, Mrs. Carson looked uncomfortable, her fan jerking nervously. "You know how people talk," she murmured. "Of course, I never listen to gossip myself but I expect it did seem odd, a young woman to die that way, so suddenly. There was talk it might have been suicide, or . . ." She flushed and fell silent.

"Murder?" I asked harshly.

The palmetto fan fluttered helplessly. "No, no, of course not. It's just, well, people can be so cruel, so thoughtless, talking without thinking. I never believed a word of it myself. Anyway it's all past now and should be forgotten."

I got to my feet and went to stand by the open window. The dimity curtains hung limp, not a breath of air stirred. The heat in the room was oppressive, making it difficult to breathe, and yet that odd chill still seemed centered deep inside my breast.

Jason Barclay hasn't forgotten, I thought. I understood now the brooding remoteness masking the homely face, the pinpoints of ice in the blue eyes. My father's face had looked like that for months after my mother's death.

Behind me, I heard Mrs. Carson replacing the glasses and pitcher on the tray. She spoke hesitantly, "You've made up your mind then, my dear? You've definitely decided to take the position at Fernwood."

I turned, surprised. "Why, yes. Is there any reason I shouldn't?"

"No. No, of course not." My landlady sighed unhappily, spoke in fits and starts. "I shouldn't say this, I know . . . I do hate meddling . . . none of my business of course . . . but with your dear father gone and your being all alone without any family to protect and counsel you, I do feel it's my duty . . ." The hands once more fluttered, despairingly. "Surely, it would be more sensible for you to return North. That aunt you spoke of in Boston . . . a young woman alone needs her family close to look after her."

I thought of Aunt Agnes, the rolls of white flesh tightly corseted, the tiny rosebud mouth that never spoke well of anyone, the thankless existence I would have, always running at her beck and call, and shook my head firmly. "I'm quite capable of looking after myself." Then, glancing suspiciously at Mrs. Carson: "You sound as if you didn't think I should accept the position at Fernwood."

Mrs. Carson looked even more flustered, if possible. "Oh, dear, no, I don't mean that, not at all. Why, I'm sure it will all be perfectly proper. Mrs. Charlotte Barclay will be there as a chaperone, and then there's another woman, too, a second cousin of Charlotte's. I never can remember her name. She's lived with the Barclays for years. They'll take good care of you. I wouldn't want you to think for a moment that I would lower myself to believe any of the ridiculous stories about a fine old family like the Barclays. It's all nasty-minded gossip, I'm sure."

But she isn't sure, I thought, looking into my landlady's unhappy face, her eyes not quite meeting mine. The truth is she's not at all sure how Celia Rougier really died.

CHAPTER THREE

For the dozenth time that afternoon, I leaned forward to look out the coach window. All I could see were storm clouds lowering overhead and dark pines wood, like a black wall, pressing in on both sides of the road. Occasionally there would be a break in the trees and a glimpse of a cleared field, a crumbling log cabin surrounded by whitewashed palings. It was the same view that had met my eyes ever since Mr. Barclay and I had left the train after a day's journey from Richmond and boarded the coach for the remainder of our trip to the Barclay plantation.

The needles of a pine branch brushed the coach window and I drew back quickly from their spiny sharpness. There was something menacing about the thick blackness of the pines, the low hanging clouds overhead, as if the coach were traveling down an unending black tunnel. And there was no turning back, even if I wanted to. I frowned impatiently, trying to shake off my gloomy mood. Why in heaven's name should I want to turn back? What lay ahead couldn't be any worse than what I had left behind. My new pupil might not be very "apt" but I had worked with dull students before. As for Mrs. Charlotte Barclay, she couldn't be any more disagreeable than my Aunt Agnes.

Determinedly I turned my glance away from the deep, black woods to my companion who was dozing in his corner of the coach, although how he could sleep with the continuous lurching of the carriage frame over the deeply rutted clay road, I couldn't imagine.

Suddenly the carriage wheels dropped with a jolt into another rut. The coach dipped sideways, flinging me abruptly against my companion before I could brace myself. Jason Barclay came instantly awake. His hands reaching out, caught me around the waist before I could tumble to the floor. At the same moment his hands tightened around me, I remembered, embarrassed, that because of the heat, I had deliberately foregone wearing my corset when I had dressed that morning. My father had never approved of the whalebone "instruments of torture" as he called them. In any case I had lost so much weight these last months that I hardly needed stays to pinch in my waist. Now, however, as I felt Mr. Barclay's grasp linger a moment longer than necessary at my waist, felt the warmth of his hands through the sheer gray merino material of my gown, I wondered uneasily what he was thinking.

Was he shocked to discover his new employee was missing one of a young lady's most common undergarments? Or was that a gleam of amusement in the cool blue eyes? It was impossible to tell. When he spoke, his voice was gruffly impersonal, as usual. "The roads are always bad this time of year. I hope you aren't too uncomfortable."

"No, I'm fine, thank you." I returned, flustered, to my own end of the coach seat, trying to adjust my hat which had been knocked over one ear, tucking a wisp of hair back into the French knot that rested uncomfortably hot on the nape of my neck. "Is it much farther?"

"Another ten miles. We'll be met at the branch road and driven the rest of the way to the plantation."

We came to another break in the pine woods, a cleared field edged with red dust-covered sassafras bushes. At the end of a road overgrown with weeds, I could see the burned and crumbling walls of what must have once been a lovely plantation home. I had seen other desolate sights like this during the last two days of my travel, hollow shells of once proud mansions, pillars entwined with ivy, blackened hulk of a chimney and nothing more.

Jason Barclay gestured toward the ruin, the stretch of empty field bristling with weeds. "Those were thriving tobacco fields once." He smiled mirthlessly. "Carpetbaggers took the land over for taxes then the broomsedge took the land away from the carpetbaggers."

"Is that what you raise at Fernwood, tobacco?"

He nodded. "Since the beginning when the first Barclay came to Virginia."

"Was that long ago?"

"Two centuries ago, at least, that's when Louis Barclay built the log house that was the first Fernwood Hall. And planted the first tobacco crop. The Indians burned him out twice, but before he died he was well on his way to owning one of the largest plantations in Virginia. It was his son, Jerome, who began building the present hall."

Once again I was fascinated by the difference in Jason Barclay's face when he talked about the plantation, at the relaxing of the stern muscles around his mouth, the warmth that touched the glacial blue eyes.

"I've been told the hall is very beautiful. How fortunate it survived the war."

"It didn't . . . not entirely. Northern troops used it as a field hospital. No doubt they would have destroyed it if it hadn't been for Giles, the overseer, who talked them out of setting a torch to the house. But they carted off most of the furniture, even tore the paneling from the walls to use as firewood."

He fell silent, his face darkening, as if his thoughts had taken a bitter turn. I didn't speak either. My own father had fought in the war on the Union side but he had seldom talked about his experiences, as if the memories were too painful. Sometimes I wondered which was worse, the horror of war itself or the bitterness of the aftermath like a lingering festering poison.

I remained silent, caught up in my own thoughts until I turned my head and discovered my companion was watching me.

He shook his head with mock gravity. "I never thought I'd find one."

"Find what?" I asked, startled.

"A young woman who didn't constantly chatter, who could sit quietly the way you do."

I smiled. "My father had a favorite proverb. Beware of the dog who doesn't bark and the woman who doesn't talk!"

Jason Barclay threw back his head and laughed. He had a deep booming laugh that bounced against the walls of the coach. "I think I would have liked your father. You were very close, weren't you?"

"Yes." I knit my hands together. It was still a shock, to remember he was gone.

"And your mother?"

"She died when I was ten. One summer when we were vacationing at the Cape, she went out by herself in a small boat. She was a good sailor; she was the daughter of an Italian sea captain. A storm came up suddenly. She couldn't make it back to shore." I fell silent, remembering the black gloom which had shrouded our house for months after my mother's death, my father's alternating wild despair and brooding withdrawal into silences no ten-year-old girl could penetrate. "Sometimes I think it would have been easier for my father if he had died with her," I said, almost to myself. "He loved her so much."

And then, aghast, I remembered that Jason Barclay had suffered a similar loss, a loved one suddenly dead in a pointless, tragic accident. How thoughtless of me to remind him this way. I stole a glance at my companion's face and saw that all the warmth and humor had drained away, leaving only a cold, brooding darkness. At least my parents had had their years of shared love. For Jason Barclay there had not even been that.

I was glad when the storm clouds which had been piled up all day, suddenly ripped open. Lightning slashed the gray underbelly of the sky and with a great crash, rain descended so suddenly that Mr. Barclay barely had time to reach around me and close the curtains of the carriage. I was aware that the coach had turned off the clay road, finally pulling to a stop at what looked like the intersection of two roads. I glimpsed through the sheets of rain a smaller carriage waiting at the side of the road.

Mr. Barclay opened his door and leaped to the ground. Forgetting maidenly modesty, I lifted my skirt around my ankles and started to follow when suddenly I felt myself being swept up from the muddy ground. Mr. Barclay's massive shoulders sheltered me from the rain as he splashed across the road, carrying me as effortlessly as if I were a mere slip of a girl. In a few seconds I was once again inside a coach, a smaller one this time with worn red velvet seats and tarnished gold tassels at the windows.

After helping the coachman transfer our few pieces of luggage, Mr. Barclay joined me in the coach. Water glistened in his red-gold hair and on his face, and his trousers were splattered with mud. But he didn't seem to mind, any more than he seemed concerned by the lightning cracking like a bullwhip overhead. Water, earth, and fire, I thought, studying my companion, the relaxed, almost sensuous look on his face, as if these were the basic elements with which he felt most at home. Then a thong of lightning struck in the woods near the carriage. I heard a tree shudder and break under the impact and I jumped, startled.

"There's no need for alarm, Miss Prentice," Mr. Barclay said calmly. "We're safe in the carriage."

Annoyed, I said quickly, "I'm not frightened of storms."

"Oh." His voice was grave but the blue eyes watching me were amused. "I thought I felt you trembling when I carried you. Naturally, I assumed it was fear of the storm."

"There was no need to . . . to carry me," I said, vexed that I was losing my composure and spoke more sharply than I intended. "I'm quite capable of managing by myself."

He laughed, that deep rumbling laugh. "I'm sure you are, Miss Prentice. I have no doubts of your capability. Perhaps it's just that Southern men aren't accustomed to such self-sufficiency in their women."

I bit my lip and fell silent, realizing how graceless I had sounded. Why must I be so . . . so prickly? Then I realized the carriage was passing between stone pillared gates, and I gazed out the window curiously. We were traveling on a narrow, gravel road, lined on either side by towering water oaks. It was early evening, too late to see clearly through the gathering dusk even if the rain had slackened. The road curved finally and I had a brief impression of openness, of a sweep of lawn, dark and shining, of rose brick walls rising before me and a gabled roof studded with a great many chimney pots.

The coach pulled to a stop. Beside me, Jason Barclay straightened and said, "Well, here we are, Miss Prentice. Welcome to Fernwood Hall."

A servant, who must have been watching for us, came hurrying down the steps. As he held an umbrella over my head, I noticed that he was elderly, his hair grizzled. Then I was hurrying up the stone steps of the house and through a lovely Georgian doorway, stepping into an oval entranceway. Someone had left a lamp with a rose-colored shade lit on an end table and the soft pink glow touched pine-paneled walls, a golden parquet floor and two large double doors on either side of the hallway.

"Jason, is that you?"

Another lamp came down the curving staircase at the end of the hall. A woman's voice behind the light was sharply questioning. Then she reached the foot of the stairs and I could see the angular features in the lamplight, a long, pointed nose and thin mouth. Pale tan hair was plaited so tightly that the skin of the face was pulled taut. "We were afraid the rain would delay you." She fell silent abruptly, noticing me for the first time.

Mr. Barclay said quickly, "Rowena, I want you to meet Quentin's new tutor, Miss Abigail Prentice. Miss Prentice, this is Miss Rowena Anderson."

This then must be the second cousin living at Fernwood, whose name Mrs. Carson could never remember. By her air of deference and yet familiarity toward Mr. Barclay, I suspected she fell into the category of poor relation. I had filled that uncomfortable position myself, the few times my father and I had been forced to live with Aunt Agnes, not to recognize the signs.

The only display of emotion the woman allowed herself was a slight upward twitch of the pale brows. "You should have let us know, Jason. I could have had a room ready." She started to turn away. "I'll fetch Aunt Charlotte. She'll want to meet Miss Prentice."

Jason Barclay's voice, oddly sharp, stopped her. "Never mind, Rowena. There's no need to disturb Mrs. Barclay. We can take

care of that in the morning. I'm sure Miss Prentice is much too
tired for formal introductions tonight. As for her room, there
wasn't time to write ahead." He added, his voice, I thought, a
shade too casual, "I thought you could put her in the room off
the upstairs veranda. That way she'll have her own private
entrance and exit from the hall."

"But that room hasn't been used in . . ." Rowena began,
startled, and then at a glance from Mr. Barclay, broke off
quickly. "Very well. I'll just put out fresh linen and light a fire."

Mr. Barclay turned to me. "I'll say good night now, Miss
Prentice. We can discuss your duties in the morning. If you're
hungry, Miss Anderson will have kept something warm for us
from supper."

He went on down the hall past the staircase to what I learned
later was a back stair leading to an upstairs wing where the Barclay men had their bedrooms. Without a word to me, Rowena
turned and started up the stairs. I followed slowly, reaching an
upper landing that appeared to dissect the house from front to
back. The spacious bedroom we entered was at the end of the
hall. An ornately carved black walnut bed with a crewel em-
broidered canopy dominated the room. The wallpaper was covered with blue roses and the satin drapes and rug were of the
same faded Wedgwood blue. The bed as well as the rest of the
furniture in the room was coated with a gray patina as if it
hadn't been polished in ages. Despite the room's look of luxury,
it had a musty, unlived-in smell and a clammy chill clung to the
air, making me even more aware of my wet clothes clinging to my
skin.

I was relieved when Rowena continued through the room to
a side door that led into a much smaller bedroom. This room
had a tiny fireplace of its own with two much-worn chintz wing
chairs and an old-fashioned rag rug on the floor by a narrow
sleigh bed. The only other furniture was a small pine wardrobe
and a dressing table. I suspected that at one time this room must
have been a dressing room for the adjoining, much grander, bedroom. A French door led out onto the veranda that Mr. Barclay

had mentioned; the only other exit evidently was through the blue room.

Rowena left and returned quickly with a basin of hot water and fresh sheets. I nodded curiously toward the next-door room. "Does anyone sleep there?"

"No," Rowena said shortly, snapping the sheets onto the bed. "Not in years. You'll be completely private here." She nodded toward the French door. "You can go out that way if you like. There's a staircase from the veranda to the garden."

After finishing the bed, she knelt and started a fire of pine cones in the small fireplace, the flame burning blue. "If you care for anything to eat . . ."

"No, thank you." I was too tired even to be hungry. All I wanted was to wash my hands and face and tumble into bed.

The woman started for the door then stopped and faced me, her voice accusing. "You're not from Virginia, are you, Miss Prentice?"

Irritation leaped inside me. Was that the way I was always to be judged, by geography? I forced myself to smile agreeably. "No, I'm not."

Rowena waited for me to continue but I saw no reason to give my life history to someone I hardly knew and who was obviously prepared to dislike me in any case. When I obstinately said nothing more, the end of the long nose pinkened and the woman turned and marched out of the room.

I dug a nightgown out of my luggage, bathed, then climbed into bed. I found myself wondering if Rowena's dislike for me went beyond the fact that I was a Yankee. Could it be because I was a woman and the other tutors had been men, possible husband candidates? In the midst of thinking this, I fell into a deep, exhausted sleep.

When I awoke the next morning, thick yellow sunlight lay like clotted cream across my bed. What time was it, I wondered, struggling sleepily into my clothes. From the hunger pangs gnawing at my stomach, long past breakfast.

I opened the French doors and stepped onto a wooden veranda, discovering that my view was not of the stately water

oaks but of a box-walled garden. Beyond the garden lay a
patch of pine woods and then a sea of green tobacco, dark
shadows rippling gently over its surface, stretching as far as my
gaze could reach. I walked across the veranda and gazed down
into the garden of Fernwood, larger and more elaborate than any
I had ever seen. Artfully planned vistas drew one's eyes to distant
restful views, or to cul-de-sacs where statuary of Greek gods and
goddesses posed languidly on pedestals. One winding brick path
led to a circular rose garden and a mottled statue of Aphrodite,
the roses allowed to grow tall and straggly, almost hiding the
statue.

The garden had obviously fallen on bad days. Weeds choked
the flower beds, unpruned shrubs leaped out of bounds, brick
walks were coated with moss. I had always managed to cultivate
a small garden wherever my father and I lived, and I felt a pang
of regret, gazing down at this beautiful but neglected garden,
like a child allowed to run wild and unkempt.

Not far from the house a red dirt road curved through the
woods into the fields, the road rising and falling with the
swelling of the land. To the right of the veranda in the distance were a cluster of vine-covered wooden shacks. Nearer
the house were several brick buildings, a kitchen with its own
vegetable garden, smokehouse, laundry house, springhouse, and
adjacent stable. The stable, built of the same rose brick as the
house, was an imposing building, which didn't surprise me. I
had already found that Southern men prized their horses next
to their womenfolk.

Curious to see what lay directly beneath the veranda, I
leaned forward against the wooden balustrade, looking down
at the flagstone terrace below. The groaning of the wood gave
me warning even before I felt the rail swaying dangerously
beneath my weight. Hastily I stepped back, for the first time
noticing that the wood of the balustrade was rotten, several of
the balusters missing.

Feeling shaken at my near mishap, I returned to the bedroom, then, driven by hunger, decided to see what I could do
about breakfast. I walked quickly through the blue bedroom.

For all its elegance, there was something about the room which depressed me, not just the dank smell of mildew but a chill in the air that despite the warmth of the morning seemed to cut through to the bone. Once outside the room, I hesitated, but there was no one in sight in the broad hallway and I continued down the staircase. Below me, sunlight streamed into the entrance hall from the fan of stained-glass windows above the doorway, and shimmered like a rainbow across the brown and gold parquet floor.

When I reached the hall, I cautiously opened the first door on my right, a heavy walnut double door with Sheffield silver doorknobs. The doors parted quietly. The drapes in this room were drawn, too, and I stepped into darkness so complete that for a moment I felt as if I had gone blind. Gradually, as my eyes adjusted to the lack of light, I became able to distinguish shapes, a row of chandeliers hanging in the vastness above me, the bulky shadows of furniture, a feeling of great space stretching before me. But it was the silence I noticed most. An impenetrable silence with the sort of thickness you felt you could reach out and touch.

Warily, I moved forward, my hands held out protectively before me—and stumbled hard against something. Almost at once I recognized what it was, a piano. I touched the keyboard. A single, bell-like note trembled in the darkness, then fell away into nothingness. The silence once more pressed in upon me.

Suddenly the quiet seemed too oppressive, the shadows of furniture like misshapen creatures crouching in the darkness. Hastily I flung open a drape covering a window twice as tall as I was. Instantly yellow sunlight sliced into the room and I saw the water oaks of the front lawn of Fernwood, casting great blue black shadows across the grass.

As I gazed out of the window, my back to the room, I felt a curious sensation on the nape of my neck, a prickling of the skin, as if someone were standing behind me. I whirled—and my heart lurched painfully.

A man in a blue velvet cape and plumed hat stared directly at me from across the room.

CHAPTER FOUR

Sunlight, tracing a path across the floor, highlighted the man's face, resembling Jason Barclay's and yet not like his at all. Although the coloring was the same, rust-red hair and deep-blue eyes, the bone structure of this face was V shaped, rather than broad, the features handsome and regular. The body beneath the blue velvet cape slung nonchalantly over one arm was as slim and sleek as a fine thoroughbred. The man continued smiling at me and yet stood as frozen in silence as I.

Then a bubble of laughter rose in my throat. It was only a portrait, a life-sized painting of a man that in the dim light I had mistaken for a real person.

I flung open another drape, letting more sunlight rush into the room. A whole row of portraits faced me. Men in old-fashioned waistcoats with perukes and women in full hoop skirts. Their glances stared haughtily over my head as if disdaining to notice me. Only the man in the cavalier's dress gazed directly at me with Jason Barclay's blue eyes.

Something about the portrait pulled me across the room to take a closer look. The artist, whoever he had been, had caught in the man's features, the posture of the figure, the slender hand resting on a sword's hilt, a sense of aliveness that was uncanny. The mouth looked as if any moment it might speak or break into laughter.

"I see brother Brian has made another conquest."

I turned, startled. A young man had come into the drawing room. As he strolled toward me, crossing the path of sunlight, I saw that his features were vaguely similar to the man in the portrait. Only the hair was a pale silver blond, the eyes more gray than blue. And although both men were slender, almost boyishly so, I sensed that the man in the portrait had a rapier's strength beneath his somewhat effete appearance which the young man before me lacked.

The young man cocked his head, amused, to one side, standing in almost the same nonchalant pose as the man in the portrait. His gaze traveled slowly from my plain black high-button shoes over my dark green poplin morning dress, still wrinkled after being hastily unpacked, to my hair pulled severely back into its usual chignon. I felt my face grow warm beneath the indifference of that gaze, slipping casually over me, as if I had been quickly judged and my charms found wanting. Then before I could move, the younger man smiled and bowed, with the automatic politeness I suspected he displayed to all elderly ladies and maiden aunts. "My apologies, Miss Prentice, if I startled you."

I have always felt uneasy with charming young men and his knowledge of my name threw me further off balance. "I . . . I don't believe we've met."

"Robert Louis Barclay, at your service," he said with a flourish. "Rowena mentioned at breakfast that brother Jason had returned from Richmond with a new tutor for Quentin. May I say, Miss Prentice, that you're a great improvement over the last two unfortunates who held that position."

I remembered then, the younger Barclay brother, the one studying law in Richmond and Mrs. Carson's disapproval. I was quite agreeable to disapproving of him, too, except I discovered it was difficult not to respond to the ingratiating charm of that smile. I found myself smiling back like any smitten schoolgirl.

Robert Barclay gestured toward the gallery. "I see you've been meeting the Barclay ancestors."

He threw open several more of the drapes. Sunlight flooded the room and I gasped with delight. A blue-white marble fireplace stood at one end of the long room, a huge gold rococo mirror above the mantel. In the mirror, a dozen gold and crystal chandeliers caught and splintered the sunlight into a thousand prisms, reflecting themselves blindingly over and over again. The floor was the same parquet as the entrance hall, dry polished till it gleamed as if with a thin coating of ice. Gold brocade drapes matched the brocade on what looked like Hepplewhite chairs. Even the ceiling and cornices were touched lightly with gold leaf, as were the frames on the portraits.

"Are they all Barclays?"

"Barclays by birth or marriage." He returned to my side, tucked my hand under his arm and we were promenading along the gallery of portraits. "That jolly-faced gentleman at the end is Louis Barclay," he intoned, much in the manner of a tour guide. "The story goes he was the young son of a noble English family who managed to escape to the colonies just a step ahead of Cromwell's men and several irate husbands. That's his son, Jerome, next to him in the fancy cape and plumed hat. He inherited Fernwood and built the hall. Unfortunately he also inherited his father's interest in the ladies. He fought a duel, killing a man over a lady's honor, a married lady unhappily. It was supposed to have happened under the water oaks just outside this room. The man he killed cursed him as he died, and two weeks later Jerome was found dead with a look of terror on his face but without a mark of violence on him."

My companion lowered his voice melodramatically. "And so the legend of the ghostly cavalier was born. Whenever he appears, a Barclay heir, male or female, is certain to die."

"How fascinating," I murmured. "But no clanking chains or moans in the night?"

He shrugged sheepishly. "Well, the truth is old Jerome probably died of a heart attack after too much overindulgence at the punch bowl, but it makes a good story and every old house worth its salt has to have its private haunt. Westover has its Evelyn Byrd, and Fernwood Hall has its ghostly cavalier."

He continued reeling off the names and lineage of each ancestor in turn until we stopped before the portrait of a heavy-set man in the uniform of an officer in the Army of the Confederacy. This man had the stockiness of Jason but his lips were thinner and there was a look of temper not too well controlled about the pale gray eyes. Rob's voice lost its mocking note, became properly respectful.

"This is my oldest brother, Guy. When he came back to Fernwood after the war, it was little more than a hollow shell. The Yankee soldiers had carted off everything they could carry, heirlooms that had been in the Barclay family for generations. They left the hall a shambles. It was Guy who devoted his life to restoring the hall to what it had been." A note of venom crept into my companion's soft drawl. "Unlike some, Guy knew the importance of gentlemen living like gentlemen, of rebuilding a way of life here at Fernwood that the war had almost destroyed."

I gestured to the portrait that had first caught my attention when I came into the drawing room. "Is this another brother?" Surely, the likeness was there. The strain of temper was in this face, too, but it was a temper curbed by the laugh lines around the mouth.

"That's Brian, Jason's twin, although as you can see, not twins in physical likeness at all. Actually Jason and Brian had very little in common, like harnessing a plow horse to a finely bred Arabian."

I doubted if Jason Barclay would be flattered at that description and I was amused at the boyish glow of hero worship in Robert Barclay's face when he stared at the portrait of his brother. "Those clothes he's wearing," I said puzzled, "don't they belong to a much earlier century?"

"It was a whim of Brian's. He thought it would be amusing to pose in the same costume that Louis Barclay might have worn, particularly since Brian seemed to have inherited his ancestor's Don Juan success with other men's wives and mistresses."

This last remark I was sure was intended to shock me, but I had read the poetry of Verlaine and Baudelaire in the original French, as well as learning the literature of my mother's homeland, and so I merely remarked thoughtfully, "I've always considered the character of Don Juan rather pathetic, a small boy constantly trying to prove what a man he is."

I was childishly pleased at the startled glance Robert Barclay gave me, as if he were really looking at me for the first time.

Then he frowned defensively. "Brian didn't have to prove himself as a man. He was more of a man than anyone I've ever met, strong, quick-witted, always filled with laughter. After he left Fernwood, the hall was never the same, as if he took all the life with him."

"Why did he leave?" I asked curiously, then bit my lip. Surely that was none of my business. I must remember that I was an employee at Fernwood Hall, not a guest of the family.

"There you are, Miss Prentice. I've been looking for you."

I had not heard Jason Barclay enter the drawing room. As I turned to face him, I realized that Robert Barclay and I were still standing arm in arm. I pulled my arm free, my voice flustered. "Mr. Barclay was showing me the family portraits."

"If you've finished." Mr. Barclay's voice was cold. "Dulcy is waiting to serve you breakfast."

"Miss Prentice was asking me about Brian," Robert drawled, and I was startled at the glittering malice in the smile he gave his brother. "Perhaps you'd like to tell her why our brother left Fernwood."

For a moment I saw the muscles around Jason's mouth harden into cords beneath the tanned mahogany skin. Then he simply dismissed his younger brother's question with an indifferent shrug. "Who knows why Brian ever did anything?" he said. He turned to me. "You'd better come along, Miss Prentice, before your breakfast gets cold."

I followed him meekly across the entranceway, through a formal dining room and into a small, adjoining sitting room. The furniture in this room was worn and comfortable-looking, the view was of the kitchen garden and a crape myrtle tree in rosy bloom.

Robert came into the room behind us, a coat slung over his arm. "I'm riding over to Twin Oaks, Jason." He gave me a quick smile. "It's been a pleasure meeting you, Miss Prentice."

"I'll expect you home for supper," Jason said bluntly. "There are some matters I need to discuss with you before you return to Richmond."

A sulky look settled around Rob's mouth. How old was he,

I wondered, probably late twenties, but he seemed much younger somehow. "Oh, very well, if you insist."

After he had gone Jason turned back to me with an absent frown. "I had hoped to discuss Quentin's schooling with you this morning, Miss Prentice, but I find we're shorthanded in the fields."

I noticed that he was wearing work clothes and that his boots were stained with red mud. I wondered how long he had been up and about while I had lain abed. I flushed apologetically. "I'm not usually such a late riser, Mr. Barclay. I'm sorry I . . ."

I was interrupted by a woman sweeping imperiously into the room through the door that led to the kitchen garden. She was dressed in black from head to toe. White hair was piled in a careful disarray of curls around a face that in youth must have had a sharply etched, imperious beauty. Even now the white skin was only slightly wrinkled around deep set, velvet brown eyes. At the moment though the eyes were flashing fire and the softly slurred voice quivered with anger as she spoke to Jason Barclay, completely ignoring me. "You must stop him at once, Jason. He's put Quentin on Firefly and I won't have it! Giles will kill the child if you don't stop him."

Almost before she stopped speaking, Jason strode through the door, with the woman close behind him. I hesitated a moment, then followed more slowly, stopping a short distance from the stable area to watch.

A young boy with bright yellow hair was mounted on a black horse in front of the stable. The boy did seem pitifully small on the back of the animal yet he was apparently in control and enjoying himself. Then the woman ran forward, calling out, "Quentin!" The boy turned his head at hearing his name. For a moment, off balance, he lost control and slipped sideways from the saddle as the horse thrust his forelegs up toward the sky.

The small body hit the ground with a soft thud. I started forward but the woman was before me, kneeling in the dust beside the boy. Quentin began to cry, much too noisily, I suspected, for any real harm to have been done. The woman hugged the boy to her, brushing at a smear of blood on the cheek. "Don't try to move, my lamb," she crooned. "Uncle Jason will carry you into the house." She cast a furious glance upward at a man standing by the stable door. "I hope you're satisfied."

The man was at least in his late fifties, but his shoulders were still broad and muscular, his shaggy blond hair only lightly touched with yellowish gray. When he spoke, he revealed a great many tobacco-stained teeth. "Hush, woman. The lad's barely bruised. A fall or two won't hurt him. How else will he learn to ride anything but ponies?"

The woman's white face grew livid with rage. She sprang to her feet, her voice trembling. "How dare you say that to me after what happened to Mr. Barclay?" She turned furiously to Jason Barclay. "I warned you this would happen. I told you to keep Giles away from Quentin."

"You're upsetting yourself over nothing, Charlotte." Jason Barclay gave his nephew an exasperated glance. "Stop yelling, Quentin, and get to your feet. You're not hurt. Only babies cry when they fall off a horse. Good horsemen get back on and ride again." Under his uncle's stern gaze, the boy reluctantly got to his feet, but made no move to remount the horse. His uncle sighed and said, more kindly, "Well, run in the house then and have Dulcy wash your face."

With a curious glance backward toward me, the boy ran off toward the house. Jason turned to the plantation manager. "I was checking the south field this morning. The worms have gotten to at least a third of it."

The man shrugged. "I told you, we're short of help."

"Well, get more workers. Maybe Sam Watkins will let us use some of his men for a few days."

"Yes, Mr. Barclay. I'll do that."

Although the words were respectful enough, I sensed a mock servility beneath the voice. There was a slyness about the milky blue eyes of the man that I disliked, particularly the way his gaze sidled over me with a ferret cunning before he picked up the reins of the black horse and turned away.

Charlotte Barclay let her breath go with an explosive gasp. "Giles takes too much upon himself, Jason. He should have been let go long ago."

"He also happens to know more about tobacco than any other man in Virginia," her brother-in-law replied curtly. "And have you forgotten, Charlotte, if it hadn't been for Giles staying on here during the war, we might have lost Fernwood."

The woman tossed her head. "I'm sick to death of hearing how much we owe Giles Latham, no better than a Yankee and a coward or he would have joined the Army like your father and brother. If Mr. Barclay were alive, he'd never allow Giles to speak to me so impertinently. He would have taken a whip to him first."

Jason Barclay smiled drily. "I doubt if even Guy would have had the nerve to take a whip to Giles. As for his interfering with Quentin, I'll speak to him about it although I fail to see what harm he's doing the boy." Then, suddenly realizing I was standing quietly to one side, he turned apologetically, "I'm sorry, Miss Prentice. You haven't met my sister-in-law yet, have you? Charlotte, this is Miss Abigail Prentice, Quentin's new tutor I've brought from Richmond."

The woman turned slowly toward me, the wide-set eyes narrowing as they stared at me. I felt a tightness like a queasiness in my stomach. For never before in my life had I encountered such a look of open hostility.

CHAPTER FIVE

Then, so quickly, I wondered later if I had imagined the whole thing, a bland politeness filled the soft brown eyes. She held out her hand to me, her voice like slowly dripping maple syrup, saying, "Miss Prentice, how very nice to meet you."

For all her frail appearance, her hand had a surprisingly firm grip. She smiled sweetly. "I understand from Cousin Rowena that your family's not from Virginia."

I could pretend to ignore that question coming from Rowena but not from the mistress of the house. "I'm from Massachusetts," I said.

"Oh." In one word she relegated that state to some outer region not worthy of further notice. "How very brave of you to come so far," she murmured. "One would assume a young lady would prefer a position closer to her home."

Mr. Barclay interceded hastily. "Since Miss Prentice will be taking over young Quentin's education, Charlotte, perhaps you have some suggestions to offer her."

Mrs. Barclay fluttered her lashes coyly. As a young woman that mannerism must have presented an appealing picture of feminine helplessness, but now seemed oddly out of place with the white hair. She shook her head. "Oh, dear, no, Jason, I wouldn't presume to give instructions to anyone as obviously competent as Miss Prentice." She made the word competent sound somehow gross. "Now if you'll excuse me, I must see to Quentin. The cut on his forehead looked bad."

She hurried away gracefully, without giving the appearance of rushing. Jason shrugged. "I warned you about my sister-in-law," he said. "Don't worry. She'll come around in time."

Never, I thought, but aloud said calmly enough: "Do you wish me to begin classes with Quentin today, Mr. Barclay?"

He glanced toward the fields, as if he were impatient to get back to his work and shook his head absently. "Tomorrow will be soon enough. I've asked Cousin Rowena to acquaint you with the house and grounds today, after breakfast, of course."

His words reminded me forcefully, along with a faint rumbling in my stomach, that I was still ravenous and it was almost noon. I returned to the sitting room where a woman with skin the blue-black color of a starling's wing placed a tray of food on a table before me, hot coffee, a plate of ham and eggs, and biscuits dripping with butter and honey. For the first time since my father's death, I ate every morsel on my plate.

After I finished, I gave a sigh of contentment. "Thank you, Dulcy," I said when the woman brought me more coffee. "That was delicious."

The woman sniffed with the familiarity of a servant who has been with a family for many years. "You look peaked to me. Nothing but skin and bones."

I laughed. "If you cook me many more breakfasts like this, I won't stay thin for long."

Dulcy straightened proudly. "I don't cook. I'm Mrs. Charlotte's personal maid. I've been with Mrs. Charlotte since her pappy bought me when I was no bigger than a bean sprout."

I was speechless. I had met very few black people in my life, much less talked to one who could speak so calmly of being bought and sold like so much merchandise. "After the war," I asked, "when you were free, you still stayed with the Barclays?"

"Where would I go?" she asked practically. "Ain't knowing nothin' but tendin' Mrs. Charlotte. How could she manage without me? Every year losing a baby, wearing herself out trying to give Marse Guy a son. Anyway, Mrs. Charlotte's been good to me. She let me keep my Dory's boy, after that traipsing child of mine ran off to the city and left him behind, let me keep Si here with me at the house, not make a field hand out of him. Ain't nothing I wouldn't do for Mrs. Charlotte."

There was a jingling noise at the door as Rowena walked

into the room. She had a metal circle attached to the belt of her dress with a multitude of keys hanging on it. In the morning light, I saw that she was younger than I had judged her to be the night before, probably not more than a few years older than I. In the bright sunlight, her eyelashes were pale gold, the eyes themselves the color of pewter, the lips narrow, compressed. Everything about Rowena seemed pulled tight, pared to the bone, spinsterish. I winced at the description. After all, I was twenty-five, teetering dangerously close to the brink of spinster-hood myself.

As instructed by Jason, she took me on a tour of the house although her attitude made it very clear that she was not happy about having to waste her time this way when she had so many other chores to do. During the tour, I couldn't help noticing that the veranda railing outside my room was not the only thing at Fernwood in need of repair. The ceiling plaster in several of the bedrooms was cracked, the paint peeling from rotting wooden window sills, the wallpaper faded and stained.

As we finished with the house and walked through the kitchen garden to the outbuildings, we passed a cold cellar, a large square hole dug in the ground. Three stone steps led down into the cellar and a wooden door fit over the opening. One side of the door was flung open and I could smell overripe fruit laid on the straw, a damp earth odor. Rowena gave a snort of irrita-tion and closed the door. "Those shiftless girls," she complained. "I've told them time and time again to keep this door shut."

In the kitchen, a separate brick building with a large fireplace in one corner and a cooking stove in the other, I met the girls, one bent, elderly woman who was the cook, and two middle-aged black women, named Bess and Lou, who had been happily gossiping when we first entered but upon seeing Rowena, promptly began working.

Rowena sighed as we left the kitchen and started back for the house. "I've told Cousin Jason over and over that it's impossi-ble to manage a house the size of Fernwood with so few servants. When Uncle Guy was alive, it was different. We had a half-dozen servants then and extra help when I needed it. But keeping up the hall isn't important these days. All the money goes to tobacco or plowing good land under and planting weeds instead of a crop."

I listened sympathetically to Rowena's grievances. Earning her keep as the unofficial and probably unpaid housekeeper for a home the size of Fernwood, I could imagine the problems she faced. And at least while I listened to her tale of woe, she seemed to forget her antagonism toward me. Once back in the house though, she said curtly, "If there's nothing else you want to see, I'll get on with my work."

"Thank you, no. I've taken enough of your time. I think I'll take another look at the library. It seems an excellent collection."

Rowena nodded proudly. "Before the war, Fernwood had one of the finest libraries in the South. The Yankees carted off most of the books though, then decided they were worthless and dumped them in the mud about a mile from the hall."

Listening to the contempt in Rowena's voice, it could have happened yesterday, I thought, as I returned to the library—Yankee soldiers living in, defiling the hall—not before Rowena was even born.

I felt more relaxed in the library and browsed happily. Some of the titles I recognized from my father's small, excellent library, the ones we had to sell along with everything else to pay for the medical bills, the expenses of the trip South. My throat tightened with remembered pain and I forced the thought away. I mustn't let myself dwell on the past. It was the present that mattered now, making a place for myself here at Fernwood, keeping my position at least long enough to earn the money to return North.

A great many of the books were gardening journals with enough dust on them to show they hadn't been touched in years. There was a complete collection of Sir Walter Scott's novels and a set of Shakespeare. To my surprise, many of the books had Jason Barclay's name in them, and I was even more surprised to discover the breadth of his reading interests, everything from a book of philosophy by Ralph Waldo Emerson to *Poems* by Emily Dickinson. Somehow it was difficult to imagine those rough farmer's hands, turning the pages of that slim book of poetry.

Finally I located some primers that must have belonged to the Barclay children when they were young, suitable, I hoped, for my classes with Quentin. I stood, books in hand, thinking about the boy. Even from that one brief glimpse, it was plain that he was overly pampered by his aunt and frightened of his uncle. Somehow during the next few weeks I'd have to chart a course between the two extremes as every good teacher must, neither too strict nor too lenient.

Then I yawned suddenly and realized, surprised, that I was still tired. Or perhaps it was the heat, a heavy, stagnant heat that followed me up to my small bedroom. The sleigh bed looked too tempting to resist. I'd lie down for a few minutes, I thought, and awoke to discover it was dusk outside, purple shadows forcing their way into my room from the veranda. As I dressed quickly, I wondered if in my position as tutor, I would be expected to eat with the family or alone. My problem was solved when Rowena knocked at the door and said Mr. Barclay had sent her to ask if I would care to join the family for the evening meal.

I thanked her and followed her down the stairs. Halfway down I realized that the door to the library behind the drawing room stood open. I could hear loud, angry voices, Robert's rather high voice complaining, "You can't expect me to live in Richmond on the pittance you send me. It's less than half what Guy allowed me. A gentleman has to maintain decent living quarters in which to entertain his friends."

"I thought you were in Richmond to study law with Judge Saxon," his brother replied coldly. "If entertainment is what you have in mind, we can use you more profitably here at the plantation."

Rowena hastily shepherded me into the dining room, away from the voices. "Poor Cousin Robert," she said dolefully, although her face held a childish, spiteful glee. "I reckon Cousin Jason will never forgive him for wanting to be a lawyer instead of a planter."

"I can't imagine that Miss Prentice is interested in private family matters, Rowena."

Rowena turned, startled, her face staining a shamefaced red. "Aunt Charlotte! I didn't see you."

I hadn't seen the woman either in the high-back wing chair by the window. Charlotte Barclay got gracefully to her small feet. Every hair of the white head was swooped into intricately formed curls so perfect they seemed sculpted into place.

As the woman glanced toward me, I instinctively braced myself. This evening, however, there was no trace of hostility in the soft brown eyes. Rather they seemed to look straight through me as if I didn't exist. She beckoned to the servant who had come into the room, the same gray-haired man who had met the carriage in the rain. "Jonas, please tell Mr. Robert and Mr. Jason that we're waiting supper."

In a few minutes the two men entered the room. I was disconcerted to discover that both men had dressed for dinner, Robert Barclay looking even more lean and dashing in his dark evening clothes, Jason tugging uncomfortably at his starched collar. I berated myself for not thinking to wear the one dress-up gown I had brought with me instead of the simple green lawn gown I was wearing.

As if guessing my discomfort, Rob smiled reassuringly across the table at me. "You're looking very lovely this evening, Miss Prentice. That shade of green is very flattering."

"Such a difficult color for most women to wear," Mrs. Barclay murmured, slipping into the chair Jason held for her. She cocked her head thoughtfully, studying my gown. "Am I mistaken, Miss Prentice, I thought I understood your father had only recently died."

I felt my cheeks grow hot at the unspoken rebuke in her voice and replied, "Father didn't believe in women wearing mourning. He made me promise not to. He said it was an outmoded pagan custom that . . ." I broke off, embarrassed, suddenly aware that Mrs. Barclay was once again wearing stark black bombazine.

She said softly, "I will never stop wearing mourning for my dear husband until the day I die."

"I'm sorry," I apologized. "I didn't mean . . ."

"Of course, you didn't," Jason said quickly. "In a way, I agree with your father. I'm afraid the South does cling too much to outmoded customs and ideas. Your Mark Twain was right when he said Southerners read too many Sir Walter Scott novels . . ."

Charlotte bridled indigantly. "How can you say that, Jason? Your own father often told me that Scott's books were models of good breeding for all young people to read."

"And what do you think of Mr. Scott's novels, Miss Prentice?" Robert Barclay asked, smiling lazily.

As a matter of fact, I had always found the novels oversentimentalized, but I wasn't about to let Robert bait me into taking sides in a family argument. I said, instead, glancing around the table: "I hadn't realized before . . . all your names are from characters in Scott's novels, aren't they?"

Mrs. Barclay nodded. "Even Jason's real name is Ivanhoe Jason Barclay." She gave her brother-in-law an annoyed glance. "And I certainly intend to see that Quentin reads all of Mr. Scott's novels."

"That might be difficult," Jason said drily, "unless that young man's reading ability greatly improves."

Then he turned the talk to tobacco for which I was grateful. Not knowing anything about the subject, I could sit back and listen. Jason mentioned that he might have to borrow more workers from Sam Watkins in the morning . . .

Robert scowled. "You'd think you'd have more pride than to ask a man like Watkins for help, no better than white trash squatting on Fernwood land."

Jason said calmly, "Haven't you forgotten that Guy sold Sam Watkins that land so he's hardly a squatter."

"Only because Fernwood was desperate for cash," Rob protested. "Guy certainly never intended to have a family like the Watkinses living so close to Fernwood Hall. We should have bought that land back years ago. That's what Brian would have done."

The expression on Jason Barclay's face flattened out into a blankness that was somehow worse than anger. His voice was terribly, icily calm. "It so happens that Brian is no longer here to manage Fernwood. I am."

My hand tightened on the fork I was holding. Tension throbbed like an invisible cord pulled taut between the two brothers, a tension that I sensed went deeper than a dispute over land rights. Rob's handsome face flushed a dull red, looking at his brother with such loathing that I shrank back in my chair, appalled.

Then abruptly he rose to his feet, staring angrily at his brother, his voice ragged with barely controlled fury. "But I'm still here, Jason. You won't find it as easy to get rid of me as you did Brian." He bowed stiffly toward his sister-in-law. "You'll excuse me, Charlotte. I seem to have lost my appetite."

He walked stiffly from the room. Jason reached for the demijohn of whiskey beside his plate and poured himself a drink. When he spoke, it was as if the ugly scene had never happened. A spark of malicious humor shone in his eyes. "By the way, Rowena, when I picked up the workmen at Sam's farm this morning, he asked me to give you his best regards."

The tip of Rowena's nose pinkened. She slid an unhappy glance toward Charlotte Barclay who said coldly, "I'm sure Rowena isn't interested in any messages from Mr. Watkins."

The rest of the meal passed in a prolonged, awkward silence with Jason drinking what seemed to me a great many glasses of whiskey. I was relieved when the meal finally finished, and, pleading weariness, I excused myself and went to my room.

I was tired but it was more of an emotional rather than a physical exhaustion. The scene at the dinner table kept returning to my mind. It was more than a family squabble. There was something ugly, frightening about the scene, the looks on the faces turned upon Jason Barclay, the hatred in Robert Barclay's, the cringing fear in Rowena's. As for Charlotte Barclay, she had been too well schooled to display any emotion except an icy hauteur toward her brother-in-law. And Jason Barclay? It was impossible to tell what he felt, or did he feel anything at all behind that cold, remote mask.

When Rowena stopped by my room after I had undressed for bed and asked if I needed anything, I assured her I didn't. "I brought some sherry," she said. "I thought it might help you sleep."

Her sallow skin was flushed. I wondered if she had sampled the sherry before bringing it upstairs.

"Thank you. Won't you join me?"

To my surprise, she accepted, sinking into one of the small, overstuffed chairs before the fireplace. It occurred to me that despite her hostile manner, she was probably lonely for feminine companionship of her own age. Her voice was fretful when she spoke. "You've no idea what it's like being buried here in the country, sometimes not seeing anyone except the servants and family for weeks on end. It's different for the rest. Aunt Charlotte is so wrapped up in Quentin, she can't think of anything else. And all Jason cares about is the tobacco. As for Cousin Rob, well, a young, unmarried man can do what he pleases."

"One of these days you'll marry," I offered consolingly. "Then you'll have a home and family of your own."

She poured herself another glass of sherry, frowning irritably. "Who can I marry?" she demanded. "Without any dowry. Oh, Aunt Charlotte would help me soon enough but Jason has control of the money in the Barclay estate and he's not about to let a penny of it go, now that he's finally gotten his hands on it. And even if I had any money, how many eligible men from good families are left in the county? Nothing but dirt farmers whose fathers couldn't read or write, who didn't own even a pickaninny before the war."

I sipped at my sherry. "Does it matter so much, the man's family?"

She gave me a scathing look. "Of course, family matters. A woman who marries beneath herself is ruined forever." She spoke so automatically I wondered if it were her own words she was using or someone else's.

"It's different for a man," she continued bitterly. "Rob can go chasing after any girl in the county, no matter who she is, and people laugh and say he's just like his brother, Brian. And Jason . . ." She broke off, giving me an uncertain, questioning glance. "Well, I don't reckon Jason will ever marry."

Deciding it was best to clear the air, I said, "I know about—about Mademoiselle Rougier's tragic accident."

And was startled when Rowena threw back her head and laughed, a shrill, vicious laugh. The pewter eyes held an unpleasant, savoring expression as they looked at me. "Accident? Is that what you've been told, that Celia's death was an accident?"

I knew then why Rowena had come to my room, not to bring me sherry or exchange girlish confidences, but to find out how much I knew about Celia Rougier's death. And I had walked right into her trap. Had Mrs. Barclay sent her, I wondered, or was it Rowena's own idea?

Well, it was too late now for evasion in any case. "I don't understand," I said, setting my sherry glass down carefully. "If the girl's death wasn't an accident, how did she die?"

The unnatural shine was even brighter in the gray eyes. Rowena leaned forward, giving me a contemptuous glance. "Why, Cousin Brian killed her, of course."

CHAPTER SIX

The moment she had spoken, Rowena glanced uneasily over her shoulder as if to make sure the door that led to the blue bedroom was closed. "I reckon I shouldn't have said that. Aunt Charlotte would be furious with me." Then with a spurious air of bravado, "Still, you were bound to hear the truth from someone. Not that there's many in the county who'd dare say anything out loud. Most of them know enough to walk softly around Jason. Besides, there aren't many families around here that haven't a skeleton or two in their own closet! Everyone knows that the O'Neill grandfather wasn't killed in a duel but a drunken brawl and that the Johnson boy turned tail and ran at Vicksburg."

I hardly listened to her stream of county gossip. So that explained the remoteness of Jason Barclay, like an invisible wall around him, not that his beloved Celia died in an accident but was murdered by his own brother. I thought of the slim man in the blue velvet cloak downstairs, the gentle curve of the mouth, the laughing eyes. It didn't seem possible he could be a cold-blooded murderer. I interrupted Rowena in midsentence. "Are you sure? How do you know it was Brian?"

Rowena shrugged. "Cousin Brian left Fernwood the same night that Celia was killed. When they found Celia dead in her room the next morning, Brian was gone and so was his stallion."

"That's hardly enough reason to accuse a man of murder," I protested.

"Oh, there was more to it than that. They knew all right."

"What about Mademoiselle Rougier's family? Why didn't they insist Brian Barclay be brought back to face trial?"

Rowena smiled thinly. "Celia had no close family. When

Jason met her in Paris, she had run away from a convent. As for an investigation, I suppose you wouldn't know, not being from around here, but the Barclays and other old families like them in the county elect the sheriff. He'd accept whatever explanation they gave him that would save the family embarrassment. Celia had caused enough trouble alive. I guess the Barclays reckoned it best to bury her quietly."

"Trouble? What sort of trouble?"

"Oh, you know the type. From the minute she walked in the front door of Fernwood, she couldn't keep her hands off any man in sight, flirting with Brian right away, and within a week, she had Rob dangling and he was only eighteen years old. She even cut her eyes at Uncle Guy who was at least twenty years older than she was. Of course, I can't say Cousin Brian tried very hard to resist her charms. It must have shook him up some when after leading him a fool's chase, Celia chose to remain engaged to Jason."

Rowena poured herself another sherry, her voice spiteful. "For myself, I've always thought that for all of Celia's sheltered upbringing, she was still smart enough to know which side her bread was buttered on. Brian had already gambled away most of his inheritance. He had nothing to offer Celia except himself."

"What happened, after Celia broke off with Brian?"

"Nothing, not right away. Brian stormed out of the house and disappeared. The day before the wedding he came back, though, drunk as a lord. He had a terrible scene with Jason, threatened to kill Jason and Celia, too, rather than see them married. I don't know what would have happened if Uncle Guy hadn't interfered. He was the only one who could manage Brian when he was drunk. Anyway no one took Brian's threat seriously. He would say and do all sorts of wild things when he'd had too much to drink, like playing the piano at all hours of the night, and once, he found an old cavalier's costume and pretended to be the ghostly cavalier, moaning and groaning and scaring everyone in the house half to death." Rowena smiled in memory. "Even Aunt Charlotte was furious with Brian that time, but no one could remain angry with Brian for very long.

"Anyway, after Uncle Guy got Brian to bed, he and Rob and Jason went to a bachelor's party at Silver Grove. Jason didn't want to go but Celia insisted. Aunt Charlotte and I went to bed early. We were both exhausted. I'd had all the work of preparing for the wedding and Aunt Charlotte had had another miscarriage a month before and still hadn't completely recovered."

"Who . . ." My throat felt dry and I took a quick swallow of my sherry. "Who found Celia's body?"

"Dulcy." A faint shine of perspiration coated Rowena's sallow skin. She ran a tongue over her thin lips and I sensed she was enjoying telling the story. "Celia was slumped over her bed, still in her nightclothes. One of Brian's dueling pistols was clutched in her hand. The pistol was from a set that had belonged to Louis Barclay and had been given to Brian when he turned twenty-one."

"Because it was Brian's gun doesn't prove he shot her," I insisted stubbornly.

Rowena blinked. "Why else should he run away in the middle of the night if he wasn't guilty? And take the other dueling pistol with him. Aunt Charlotte saw him leave. It was several hours after she had gone to bed. Her bedroom is at the other end of this hall, looking out over the front drive. Hoofbeats awakened her and she went to the window and saw Brian riding his chestnut stallion down the road as if the devil were at his heels."

"How terrible for Mr. Barclay," I murmured. How he must have reproached himself, I thought, for leaving Celia alone that night.

"I've never seen a man so beside himself," Rowena agreed. "Jason locked himself in the library and wouldn't see or talk to anyone. It was Uncle Guy and Aunt Charlotte who had to make the decisions about Celia's funeral, where she would be buried, even what she would be buried in. All her clothes were already packed in her Saratoga trunk. She and Jason had planned to leave on a two-month wedding trip immediately after the ceremony. The trunk was locked and neither Aunt Charlotte nor I could find where Celia had placed the key. All there was left in Celia's wardrobe was her wedding gown and some calico and muslin housedresses, not fancy enough to take along on her honeymoon. So she was buried in her wedding gown and Uncle Guy decided it would be best to burn Celia's trunk, get rid of everything that would remind Jason of her. But then Jason didn't even go to the funeral. He simply left Fernwood for a year, no one knows where. When he came back, he was . . . different."

"Different? How?"

Rowena frowned uncertainly. She obviously wasn't used to dissecting character. "Just different, more quiet, moody, not that he'd ever been a gadabout or ladies' man like his brother. Jason had always been the stick-in-the-mud, with his nose in a book, clumsy, falling over his feet. Now all he was interested in was the plantation, new ways to raise tobacco. I remember Uncle Guy and he used to have terrible arguments about what sort of tobacco to grow, the old dark leaf for chewing tobacco or the yellow, sun-cured tobacco leaf they're putting in those new cigarettes they're making down in Carolina. Uncle Guy liked doing things the way they'd always been done, and, of course, he always won the arguments because he was the oldest brother."

I wasn't interested in hearing about tobacco growing and impatiently pulled the subject back to Celia's death. "Didn't anyone in the family try to find Brian?"

Rowena shook her head. "With all the gossip circulating about Celia's death, the family thought it best to let Brian drop out of sight completely. But I always suspected that Giles kept in touch with him. He and Brian were thick as thieves and Giles used to visit down in New Orleans two or three times a year. I always thought that's where Brian went and I was right," she added triumphantly.

"That's where Brian died, isn't it, New Orleans?"

Rowena nodded. "Two years later, Giles came back from one of his trips to New Orleans with young Quentin, just a baby, in his arms. He had a letter from Cousin Brian to Uncle Guy. He knew he was dying and he asked that Guy would look after his wife and child, but it was too late for Brian's wife.

She died a few hours after Brian. Brian's last request was that his son be raised at Fernwood so Giles brought Quentin back with him."

Rowena gave a brittle laugh. "Not that there was any argument about Quentin belonging at Fernwood. I'll never forget the look on Aunt Charlotte's face when they put young Quentin in her arms. She had had another miscarriage a few months before and the doctors told her she could never have a child of her own. She was half out of her mind with grief. The doctor always said young Quentin saved Aunt Charlotte's sanity."

"And Mr. Barclay?" I asked curiously. "How did he feel about accepting Quentin?"

"There wasn't anything Cousin Jason could say, was there?" Rowena asked practically. "After all, Quentin was a Barclay. Even Cousin Jason couldn't leave him to be reared by strangers."

Every time he looks at the boy though, I thought uneasily, does Jason Barclay remember the father? Wouldn't that explain his coldness toward the boy? Yet, strangely enough, I found it wasn't Jason I felt sorriest for but Brian Barclay. I remembered the proud set of the shoulders in the portrait, the possessiveness in his glance as he looked out across the drawing room of Fernwood. How it must have wounded a man of his pride to flee Fernwood like a thief in the night, to die an outcast with the guilt of a young girl's violent death on his conscience.

In the hall I heard the grandfather clock strike and Rowena turned her head toward the sound then rose, a little unsteadily, to her feet, her voice slurred. "It's late, I must go. I'm afraid I've been talking too much."

There was one last thing I still had to know though, something that bothered me about Celia's death. "Why didn't anyone hear the shot that killed Celia? Why didn't they investigate right away?"

"She was killed while the men were still celebrating at Silver Grove," Rowena explained. "Giles naturally doesn't sleep in the house. He has quarters over the stable." She hesitated. "In any case, he had gone to New Orleans on a buying trip. He didn't return until the next day. As for Aunt Charlotte and me, our bedrooms are at the other end of the hall. The walls of Fernwood are thick. We couldn't have heard any noise from here."

"Here?" Startled, I half rose to my feet.

Rowena paused in the doorway, swaying a little and smiling guilelessly. "I forgot, you didn't know, did you? Celia had the blue bedroom. Your bedroom used to be her sitting room." She opened the door behind her and some of the coldness, the clamminess of the adjoining bedroom crept into my tiny room. "Jason insisted she should have the finest room in the hall, and that her bedroom must be kept filled with roses, fresh each morning. He was besotted with her, of course. Poor Jason."

Reluctantly I came to stand beside her, gazed into the darkened room, the huge bed a darker shadow than the rest. Almost, for a moment, I could imagine I saw the white body of Celia slumped across that bed, the blood staining the coverlet.

Rowena lifted her lamp, ran a housewifely finger down a dusty rosewood dressing table and made an annoyed mouth. "It's impossible to get the girls to clean in here. They absolutely refuse. They believe she's still here, you know . . . here in this room." Her eyes looked uneasily away from mine. "Nonsense, of course. Still, sometimes . . ." She laughed nervously, an edge of malice in her voice. "You're not superstitious, I hope."

"No," I said slowly.

"That's good. I'll leave you to get your rest now. Breakfast is at seven."

After she had left, I decided that I had been mistaken, thinking that the housekeeper and I could become friends. I would have to be on guard against Rowena, the hidden malice in her that could strike out at you when you least expected it. I was sure she had told me of the servants' fear of the blue room simply to upset me, to frighten me.

Well, I didn't frighten that easily, I thought, climbing into my narrow bed, my mouth setting stubbornly. Yet that night I didn't fall asleep immediately, despite my weariness. I tossed and turned, my thoughts always coming back to Celia Rougier and her tragic fate. Perhaps it was because Celia, like myself, had been a "foreigner," an outsider, coming to Fernwood. I wondered how she had felt. Was she frightened, uncertain of her welcome? Or had she been as Rowena described her, too shallow and vain to be concerned about what others thought of her.

I twisted restlessly, trying to find a comfortable position. Unfortunately there were too many pieces missing to picture Celia clearly in my mind. I wasn't even sure I could trust Rowena's unflattering description of the French girl. Rowena would undoubtedly have been resentful of any beautiful young woman who came to Fernwood. And there was something else wrong, too, with Rowena's story, something that kept nagging at a corner of my mind until at last I fell asleep.

Almost immediately it seemed I began to dream, rather a series of dreams. First, a woman alone, dressed all in white, waltzing round and round all alone in an enormous empty drawing room like a figurine on a music box. She turned so quickly that I could not glimpse her face. Then very slowly the music began to run down. The woman's arms and shoulders drooped, and finally I saw her full front. She had no face. And to my horror, the bodice of the white gown was stained scarlet, a crimson rose pinned to her breast.

Then, in the manner of dreams, the woman dissolved and it was a man walking down the long, dark drawing room toward me. He wore a plumed hat and velvet cape tossed carelessly over one arm. Oddly enough I felt no fear. I simply stood, waiting. Now he was so close I could see his face clearly, Brian Barclay's face. His hands lifted beseechingly toward me were covered with blood; his face held such a heart-rending look of despair that I cried aloud, and woke myself up.

This was ridiculous, I thought, staring sleeplessly into the darkness around me. I had to have a good night's rest. Tomorrow was my first day working with young Quentin and the first teaching day is always the hardest. I would need all my wits about me. Perhaps some warm milk would help.

I slipped into a loose, white robe, took the lamp beside the bed and with the wick turned low, went quietly down the stairs, my feet making no more than a hushed whisper over the worn carpeting. I was almost at the foot of the staircase when I became aware of a dark figure standing in the darkness below me. I heard a sharp indrawn breath, a sigh of fear or despair, quickly silenced. Then Jason Barclay's voice lashing out angrily, "What the devil do you think you're doing?"

The abruptness of our meeting, the harshness in his voice threw me off balance. I stumbled on the lower step and he caught my arm, took the kerosene lamp into his own hand to keep it from falling. The grip of his fingers cut cruelly into my arm, but his voice, though still taut, became more civil. "You shouldn't be wandering around the house at night, Miss Prentice. Is anything wrong?"

"No . . . nothing," I stammered. I saw that he was still in his dinner clothes but he had taken off his jacket and his shoulders strained against the white cambric shirt he wore. He smelled of whiskey and tobacco and in the lamplight his eyes had a dazed expression, like a sleepwalker not completely awakened. I spoke more quickly as I regained my composure. "I couldn't sleep. I thought I'd fix myself some warm milk. I'm sorry if I startled you."

He shook his head, as if shaking away a bad dream. "My fault . . . for a moment I thought . . ." He stepped back, his hand falling away from my arm. "I must be more tired than I realized." He smiled wryly. "Or had one too many whiskeys. Jonas is still up. I'll have him bring you the milk. Though it seems a hot night for such a remedy for sleeplessness."

The lower part of his body was hidden in shadows but in the lamplight I could see his face clearly. And it suddenly, uncomfortably occurred to me that he could see me just as clearly, and that a nightgown and robe were hardly proper attire in which to carry on a conversation with my employer.

I felt as if the lamplight were burning my skin and I turned away hastily. "Thank you. I'm sorry to be a bother."

"No bother," he assured me gravely. "I was up late working on the books. I confess that's one part of running a plantation I could do without. Unfortunately old Giles is no better with figures than I am."

Impulsively I turned back, spoke without thinking. "Father

always said I had a good head for figures. If you'd like, perhaps I could help you with your bookkeeping."

"That's kind of you, Miss Prentice, but I think you'll have your hands full enough with young Quentin." He laughed softly, and suddenly, unexpectedly reached up to lightly brush my hair, hanging loose to my shoulders. "You know, at the moment though, you don't look old enough to be teaching anybody."

For a moment only the hand lingered but it was a moment I would not try to measure in time. All I knew was that the brooding look of sadness was all at once gone from Jason Barclay's face. His eyes on mine were warm and yearning, as stripped and vulnerable as a young boy. I felt a sharp ache near my heart, something stirring, a thrusting to life I had never felt before.

Perhaps my feelings showed on my face. I have never been good at hiding my emotions. And Jason Barclay's hand awkwardly fell away, the skin, roughened, catching in my hair then pulling free. I heard him take again that odd, harsh breath, his voice once more gruff, "You'd better return to your room, Miss Prentice. I'll see that Jonas brings you your milk."

I took my lamp and fled up the stairs, but very much aware of the man standing at the foot of the stairs, staring after me.

Ten minutes later Jonas, climbing the outer stairs, brought me a cup of warm milk. But even after I drank the milk and returned to bed, it was much, much later before I finally fell asleep.

CHAPTER SEVEN

Despite the lack of sleep, I felt surprisingly rested when I awakened the next morning, and I was humming to myself as I dressed quickly and hurried downstairs. When I reached the dining room, however, I found only Rowena at the breakfast table, and I fought back a stab of disappointment. How early did Jason Barclay eat, I wondered.

Rowena patted her thin lips and carefully replaced her napkin. "Aunt Charlotte said to tell you Quentin will be ready for his lessons at nine, when they return from their morning ride."

Her voice was irritable as if she were annoyed with herself for having talked so much to me the night before. I saw the table was set for only four and at my questioning glance, she added shortly, "Cousin Robert left for Richmond last night, and Cousin Jason usually has an early breakfast in the kitchen. You'll excuse me. I have work to do."

After I finished breakfast, I went into the small sitting room next to the dining room where I planned to hold lessons. Quentin arrived promptly at nine o'clock, along with a young Negro boy who slipped into the room without a word and sat quietly in a corner. Before I could speak, Quentin said, "That's Si. He goes everywhere I go. The other tutors always let him come to class with me."

I vaguely remembered then that Si was Dulcy's grandson but I was too eager to have the lessons start well to protest an extra pupil. "That's fine," I said, giving Quentin a friendly smile. At least it was friendliness on my part; I wasn't sure about Quentin. He showed no outward hostility toward me but his pale blue gaze was like quicksilver that never stayed in one place for long. And he very seldom looked directly at me.

"I hope we'll be good friends, Quentin, as well as teacher and student," I said, indicating where he should sit.

He shrugged indifferently, his gaze slipping away from me, the sunlight making a misleading halo around his blond head.

"Aunt Charlotte said I had to come or Uncle Jason would jump on me."

"Your Uncle Jason is anxious for you to have an education," I said. "You have a good library here at Fernwood. Don't you like to read?"

Again the bored, indifferent shrug. "I don't know how to read." Then, defiantly, "I could if I wanted to but I don't want to."

I tried not to show my shock at his words. Eight years old and not able to read! "I'm sure you could," I said. "And I should think you'd want to. After all, someday you will be head of Fernwood Hall. How will you be able to run a plantation if you can't read or do figures?"

"Oh, I'll have servants to do stuff like that," he said carelessly. "Giles never went to school but a few years and he says it never hurt him any."

"Perhaps if Mr. Latham had an education, he would own a plantation instead of working for someone else," I replied tartly. Before Quentin could reply to that, I added hastily, "Now let's see how much you do know. You know your alphabet, don't you?"

The rest of the morning was spent discovering to my dismay how little formal education Quentin did have. And how difficult it was going to be to reach the boy. His mind was quick enough when he wanted it to be but his attention was as difficult to hold as a wiggling puppy. If I didn't watch him every minute, his gaze would drift dreamily out the window, his thoughts obviously miles away.

By the end of the morning I was exhausted and decided to forego any attempt at afternoon lessons. Instead, I asked Quentin if he would like to show me around the plantation, at least as much as we could see on foot.

"Don't you ride, Miss Prentice?" he asked, surprised.

"Not very well," I admitted. "Perhaps someday you can be the teacher and show me how to improve my horsemanship."

He looked pleased at the thought and while we walked down the road away from the hall, toward the tobacco fields . . . with Si following us like a shadow dogging our footsteps . . . he chattered happily about the horse his Uncle Jason promised to buy him as soon as he was twelve years old.

A rail fence almost completely entangled in creepers edged the dirt road; the orange flowers of the vine lifted like a multitude of silent trumpets to the bleached blue sky. Beyond the fence in an abandoned field the brittle flowers of life-everlasting mingled with ragweed and broomsedge blazing beneath the August sun.

We finally crossed a narrow wooden bridge spanning a pond. Willows and bent black pines held back the sunlight and the surface of the pond lay in shadows, dark and still. Cattails grew in the water, bullfrogs croaked hoarsely and dragonflies hovered over the unsightly green scum coating the edges of the pond.

"That used to be our ice pond," Quentin said. "We don't use it for that any more."

He was walking faster and talking less as we followed a bend of the road curving down into a hollow away from the pond. Finally he stopped talking altogether.

"What's that?" I asked curiously, pointing toward a square brick-walled enclosure a short distance from the road.

"That's the family burying ground," Si answered for Quentin.

"But the gate's walled shut!"

Si cast a glance at the silent Quentin, trudging ahead, then mumbled, "No more room, ma'am. It's done filled up. Marse Quentin's pappy . . . he was the last one. They shipped him all the way up from N'Orleans." His eyes widened, fascinated, at the thought.

Appalled, I looked quickly toward Quentin, at the boy's thin shoulders hunched forward, the narrow collarbones sticking out like plucked wings. A wave of self-reproach engulfed me. Why hadn't I thought sooner how it must be for Quentin? Surely he must have heard the rumors about the death of Celia Rougier and his father. What a weight for those young shoulders to bear, not only that his father had died a disgraced exile but a murderer as well. I would like to have put my arms around those hunched shoulders but I didn't dare. We were too newly acquainted. I would have to win his friendship first.

We had come to the edge of the tobacco fields. Workers moved slowly between the rows of emerald leaved plants, bending then straightening carefully. Here and there a pink flower swayed in the breeze like a pink sail in a sea of green. "What are those men doing, Quentin?" I asked.

"Why, they're removing the suckers and pinching off new growth," he said, as if surprised at my stupidity. "All tobacco's got to be suckered and topped and primed."

At my blank look, he continued patiently. "That way you get eight or ten prime tobacco leaves to a stalk, and by cutting off the flower, you stop the plant from going to seed. Only you got to step real careful, not to bruise the stalks or leaves."

"Is school out for the day, Miss Prentice?"

I hadn't heard Jason Barclay come up the road behind us and I whirled, feeling all at once ill at ease, remembering last night, those rough hands stroking my hair. But there was no glimpse of that memory in Mr. Barclay's chill blue eyes and his voice was pleasantly polite, nothing more.

"Quentin was explaining tobacco growing to me," I said, feeling somehow let down and even more annoyed at myself for feeling that way. Quentin had spotted Giles and he raced off to the man who swung him up in his arms with a whoop of laughter. "I had no idea there was so much labor involved."

Mr. Barclay gazed out across the field, his voice sober. "It takes one man to tend two or three acres of tobacco. That same man could cultivate twenty acres of wheat or corn. That's why, even with slave labor, tobacco was an expensive crop. Not to mention that in a matter of years, tobacco leaches all the good out of the soil, ruins it for future planting. When my brother, Guy, was alive, I kept trying to get him to try a different crop, to bring the soil back. But he wouldn't listen; most planters around here prefer the old ways. It's only since his death that

I've been able to put nitrate and sulphates back into the land, sow cowpeas and turn them under to enrich . . ."

He broke off apologetically. "Forgive me, Miss Prentice. I'm sure young ladies aren't interested in the trials and tribulations of a farmer's life."

I found though that I was interested, listening intently to Mr. Barclay's every word. I wanted to ask more questions but the overseer came up just then and said Mr. Barclay was needed at the curing sheds. Then with a leering smile toward me: "That is, if Miss Prentice can spare you."

I felt a flush rise in my cheeks and decided that Mrs. Barclay was right. The man, Giles, was insolent and rude. Why did Jason Barclay put up with him?

Still, there was no way I could prolong the conversation and, calling Quentin, I made as graceful a withdrawal as possible.

After that first morning, my days at Fernwood fell into a set pattern, morning classes with Quentin and Si, a long noon break and then another brief class before supper. I was given a horse, a gentle mare, to ride but it was evident I wasn't a good enough horsewoman to keep up with Mrs. Barclay and Quentin on their morning rides, even if I didn't suspect that Charlotte resented sharing her time with Quentin with another person.

In the evening after supper, Mrs. Barclay would work at her needlework and Rowena attended to the darning while Jason glanced through the newspapers sent by mail from Richmond. Since I have never had much aptitude for the needle, I usually selected a book from the library to read. Occasionally Jason would read aloud some item from the newspaper, usually something light, or news of a social happening. One evening though, having glimpsed a portion of the front page, I asked him for news of the economic depression that was sweeping the country. Fear of a full-scale recession had already had Boston in its grip when Father and I left the city months before, with banks and railroads collapsing and failing, falling like dominoes one after another.

"When I was in Richmond earlier this month I read that President Cleveland was calling a special session of Congress to consider the crisis," I commented. "There was talk he was going to ask for the repeal of the Sherman Silver Purchase Act in order to maintain our gold standard. There was even a rumor that several banks were near to closing in Richmond."

Mrs. Barclay glanced up sharply. "Crisis? What crisis is that, Jason? Surely our bank in Richmond is perfectly sound."

"Of course, Charlotte," Mr. Barclay said quickly, too quickly I thought. "Don't concern yourself. It's just one of those periodical financial upsets that the government gets itself into. It'll straighten out soon enough." He gave me a patronizing smile. "Miss Prentice has misunderstood the situation. The President will surely realize the futility of continuing to back our silver dollars with gold. He'll only end up antagonizing the Western miner and the Southern farmer if he insists on maintaining the gold standard, with gold the government doesn't even have."

I frowned, annoyed at his condescending tone of voice. I wasn't any financial expert but Father and I had had long discussions on the subject and before I came to Fernwood I had always read the newspapers carefully. "Going off the gold standard would reduce the value of the dollar to fifty cents, Mr. Barclay," I pointed out tartly. "Surely you wouldn't want that to happen. Think of the hardship that would cause the workingman with his small savings cut in half overnight."

And thus began the first of several heated discussions between Mr. Barclay and myself over the next weeks, ranging from the economic problems facing the country, to whether the government had had the right to send American Marines to Hawaii, thus bringing about the annexation of that small island kingdom, even touching upon the morality of the workingman's right to strike for better wages.

During our discussions, Rowena and Charlotte always sat quietly, until one evening Mrs. Barclay cleared her throat disapprovingly—after I had made a particularly vehement objection to a stand Jason Barclay had taken—and said firmly, "No doubt, Miss Prentice, a man understands these subjects better. I find it's dangerous for a young lady to concern her mind with such things."

Jason shrugged and gave his sister-in-law a wry smile. "I don't believe we have cause to worry about Miss Prentice's mind, Charlotte. It has an uncomfortably sharp edge."

I went to bed that night, not sure whether I had been insulted or flattered. Then scolded myself for caring either way. It was just that I was lonely here at Fernwood, I told myself. After being my father's close companion for so many years, I missed a lively conversation, the thrust and parry of a good argument. Not that my father and Jason Barclay were anything alike. My father had been ascetic looking, frail and scholarly, while Jason . . . I thought of that face, the rudely shaped features; the heavy body with its almost clumsy gait, those large rough hands. And yet I remembered how gently, how effortlessly those hands had lifted me, carried me to the carriage, making me feel small, somehow infinitely precious . . .

Lying in my narrow bed, watching a harvest moon spill like fluid gold across the floor of my room, I felt a dangerous warmth seep through my body, an aching yearning for what I didn't know, a restlessness that pulled at my nerves and made it difficult to sleep. Finally I went to stand out on the veranda, welcoming the slight cool breeze that stirred the fern-like branches of the mimosa tree below me. Then beyond the few tufts of pink blossoms still blooming, I saw a pinpoint of red light move in the garden, and recognized the figure of Jason, smoking a cigar, taking a last stroll in the garden before turning in.

I thought for a moment he looked up toward the veranda where I stood and I stepped back, trying to merge my white nightgown with a pillar. I was sure though he had seen me. What was he thinking, I wondered. Was he too restless to sleep, too? Suppose he should climb up the outer staircase with that heavy, ponderous tread, come to stand beside me, span those hands around my waist . . . I didn't allow myself to think any further. Turning, I fled back into my bedroom, pulled the thin coverlet over me, trembling as if I were all at once chilled. What was happening to me, I wondered panic-stricken.

I wasn't some moonstruck child. I had always prided myself on my common sense, of looking facts full in the face. And the first fact, of my own unattractiveness, I had learned very early in life, the way people usually learn unpleasant facts about themselves, by inadvertently eavesdropping on a conversation between my father and my Aunt Agnes when I was fourteen.

My aunt was complaining to my father, as usual, about what she considered my outlandish upbringing. "What sort of husband will that girl ever get, after you've filled her mind with all sorts of nonsense. Goodness knows, she's not pretty. It'll be difficult enough for her to make a good match."

My face burning with anger, I waited for my father to defend me, to say that it was a lie, that I was pretty, but he only said, placidly enough, "Oh, I'm not worried about Abby. She has good instincts and a lively, intelligent mind. She's beautiful in spirit, if not in body. What if she doesn't marry? There's no great shame in a woman remaining single."

I turned over, burying my flushed face in my pillow at the memory. There was a shame though my father hadn't mentioned, the shame of yearning for a man who was already bound in spirit if not in flesh to someone else, a woman dead for ten years now but whose presence I could still feel in the elegance of the blue bedroom, like a fragile, lovely scent that would not fade from the air.

The next day I threw myself more vigorously into my teaching duties, determined to put all thought of Jason from my mind. During the morning, however, I had to leave the sitting room for a few minutes and when I returned, I found both Quentin and Si gone.

Exasperated, I began looking for the truants. Quentin wasn't in his bedroom which was next to his aunt's, but as I came out into the upstairs hall, I noticed the door to the attic was standing ajar. I peered up the wooden staircase, a wave of hot air rushing down out of the cavernous darkness above me. Then I thought I heard footsteps and picking up my skirt so the hem wouldn't trail in the dust on the stairs, I climbed quickly upward.

The attic wasn't completely dark. I could distinguish pieces of discarded furniture, old pictures, chests shoved untidily along the walls, all the flotsam and jetsam from generations of Barclays who had once lived and died at Fernwood.

To young boys like Quentin and Si, the attic would seem a wondrous place to play and hide, but I was only conscious of the unbearable heat, trickles of perspiration running down my back. A rustling noise made me jerk around before I realized it must be squirrels running on the roof—or rats, I wondered uneasily, lifting my skirt higher.

I stood perfectly still, listening for the revealing sound of a young boy's giggle but could hear only my own breathing. Around me there pressed the same thick silence I had felt that first morning in the drawing room, the sense of eyes watching me, dark and malignant, waiting in the shadows.

Irritated at my fancies, I started quickly down the aisle between a row of trunks to a gabled window, when my eye was caught by one of the trunks, smaller than the others, shoved into a corner, almost hidden from sight. I wouldn't have noticed it at all if the sunlight slanting through the windows hadn't glinted on a pair of gold entwined initials engraved on the Saratoga trunk.

Incredulously my hand reached out to trace the initials with my fingers—*CR*. Celia Rougier. My lips soundlessly formed the name.

"Miss Prentice? Whatever are you doing up here?"

Rowena walked toward me, a white apron tucked all around her skirt to protect her dress, a smudge of dirt on her cheek.

I gestured, startled, toward the trunk. "Isn't that Mademoiselle Rougier's trunk? I thought you said it had been burned."

Rowena frowned, correcting me. "I said Uncle Guy wanted it burned but naturally Aunt Charlotte had too much sense to burn perfectly good clothes. We put the trunk up here in the attic where it would be out of Jason's sight. I'm sure Aunt Charlotte meant to have the lock forced open one day but I suppose she forgot all about it. I know I did." She gave me a sharp glance. "You haven't said what you were looking for up here."

I explained about Quentin's disappearance and she quickly

shook her head. "He's not up here, or I'd have seen him. I've been hanging lavender to dry. If Quentin's playing hooky, I'd suggest you look in the stable. He always runs off to Giles every chance he gets."

"Thank you," I said, pretending not to notice her disapproving glance which said clearly: How do you expect to teach the boy if you can't even keep him in class with you?

I left the house and walked reluctantly toward the stable. The stable was Giles Latham's domain and I stayed away from the place as much as possible so as not to run into the man. Still, I knew if I let Quentin get away with slipping out of class once, it would be that much harder to control him the next time.

The darkness of the stable after the bright sunlight momentarily blinded me. It took several seconds before I could make out bridles hung on the wall, a lantern, an old-fashioned Inverness cloak like my father used to wear but much more worn, and next to the cape what looked like a coiled piece of rope. One of the horses in his stall nickered softly, stretching out his head as if to greet me.

I crossed over to him, reaching out to stroke the black velvet nose when a hand roughly grabbed my arm, a voice saying, "I wouldn't touch him if I was you, not if you want to keep your fingers."

CHAPTER EIGHT

I jerked my hand away and turned to face the plantation manager.

"What . . . what a beautiful animal," I said. I heard the stammer in my voice and took a deep, angry breath. Why should I let this man frighten me? "He's new, isn't he?"

"You'd best stay clear of him," Giles warned. "He's got a mean streak. He almost killed his last owner."

I stepped back a little but not before I noticed the ugly marks across the animal's flank. "Why, this animal's been mistreated," I said indignantly. "Those are whipmarks."

Giles shrugged. "Young Rob won him in a poker game in Richmond, had him sent down here the other day. I guess the man who owned the stallion thought he could break the beast. I could have told him he was wasting his time. A stallion with that look in his eye is nothing but trouble." He scratched his chin reminiscently. "Same way with the young bucks I bought before the war. One look and I could tell whether they'd settle down or be troublemakers." He looked over my shoulder, smiling, and something about that self-satisfied smirk sent a shiver down my spine. "Of course, there weren't many, man or beast, I couldn't break, one way or the other, given time."

I followed his gaze to the wall of the stable where a thonged whip hung, gathering cobwebs now but still vicious looking. I swallowed hard and looked away from those milky blue eyes with their feral cunning.

"This is all very interesting, Mr. Latham, but I really came here, looking for Quentin." I thought I heard the sound of a nervous titter from a corner behind a pile of saddles and I raised my voice as I turned and walked to the door. "It's too bad I can't find him. I was planning to read him a story, one of his favorites."

What a vile man, I thought, as I walked slowly back to the house, rubbing my hands along the skirt of my gown as if to rid them of some invisible filth. What was even worse, I suspected Giles Latham was not a stupid man. Even his half-educated way of talking I had the feeling was put on, a way of hiding his intelligence while secretly laughing at those who underestimated him.

I stopped at the kitchen for a cooling drink of water then returned to the sitting room. I found Quentin and Si waiting for me, a look of sweet innocence on both their faces. Taking my chair, as if nothing were amiss, I said, "As soon as we've finished our arithmetic lesson, I'll read a story to you. Was there any particular one you'd like to hear?"

Si, who seldom spoke, piped up eagerly, "A hant story, Miss Abigail. Would you read us a hant story?" Then he gave Quentin a sly, teasing glance. "'Cept maybe hant stories scare some folks."

Quentin flushed angrily. "You say I'm scared and I'll hit you."

I intervened hastily. "I'm sure Quentin isn't frightened of hants, Si. He knows there's no such thing as a ghost."

"Why, yes, there is, Miss Abigail," Si said, startled. "Ain't you never seen a hant?"

"No, and neither has anyone else."

"Uncle Jonas did," Si insisted. "He seen the hant by the bury hole the night before Marse Guy fell off his horse, looking jes like his picture 'cept his hands all bloody and that's the truth. Marse Quentin's seen him, too, ain't you?"

Quentin said nothing. I was shocked when I saw the boy's face, the blue eyes enormous, the small mouth pinched with fear.

Remembering a book of Washington Irving stories I had seen in the library, I said hastily, "If you study hard the next hour, I'll read you both a story about a headless horseman who once lived in the Catskill Mountains in New York."

I saw I had their undivided attention now and for the rest of the day I had no more trouble. I thought that I had handled the whole matter of the boys' truancy very well until that evening after supper. Instead of the sitting room, we had coffee that night in the drawing room, with the gold-embroidered Hepplewhite chair making a perfect foil for Charlotte Barclay in her black widow's weeds. Smiling sweetly, she looked up from her embroidery and said, "I saw Quentin running out to the stable this morning, Miss Prentice. I thought he was supposed to be at lessons with you."

A flush climbed my cheeks but before I could reply, Jason looked up from his newspaper, his voice gruff. "Are you having trouble with that young man? If so, tell me and I'll have a talk with him."

"No," I said quickly. "That won't be necessary." If I had to rely on Quentin's fear of his uncle to gain control of him, then I knew I had failed as a teacher. Seeking for a change of subject, my gaze lit on the rosewood piano. "I was thinking, though, that I might try and teach Quentin something of the piano. Not that I'm a trained pianist, but I can play a little, and Quentin does seem to have a natural musical talent."

I was shocked at the reaction to my innocent remark. Jason was on his feet, glaring down at me, his voice, grating, "I'm not interested in your turning the boy into a damn music master, Miss Prentice. I would think you have enough on your hands just teaching him to read and write."

Then he strode off into the library, leaving me, I'm afraid, with my mouth half ajar in surprise at the storm that had unexpectedly broken over me.

"Oh, dear," Mrs. Barclay said softly. "I should have warned you, Miss Prentice. No one plays the piano at Fernwood any more. Not since . . ." She hesitated, then began again, "Not since Quentin's father left." She sighed and shook her head. "It does seem a shame, too. The Barclays were a very musical family at one time. All the children were taught the piano but Brian was the gifted one."

I remembered then, Rowena's telling me that sometimes Brian Barclay came home drunk and played the piano at all hours of the night. Naturally, Jason wouldn't be too happy to see Quentin following in his father's footsteps, and the sound of the piano being played could only bring back unhappy memories.

Mrs. Barclay picked up her embroidery and bent her white sculptured curls. "How sad that the drawing room should never be filled with music again. When I remember the way it was before the war, the grand balls that were held in this room. It was the one dream of my husband's life, you know, to return Fernwood to the showplace it once was. Unfortunately, Jason has little interest in such things. The hall has gone dreadfully downhill these last years."

I was only half listening; my thoughts were on Jason, still shaken by the memory of the anger that had struck his face, distorting the usually calm, familiar features into a violent landscape I no longer recognized. I excused myself as soon as possible and went to bed early that night and fell asleep, dreaming of how Fernwood must once have looked, ablaze with candlelight, beautiful ladies in crinolines waltzing like gay flowers caught in the arms of handsome cavaliers, music flowing through the windows out beneath the water oaks.

When I awoke, my dream was so real that I thought I could still hear the music playing. Then I sat bolt upright in bed. It wasn't music that had awakened me. It was the sound of a child's terrified screams.

Without even bothering with my robe, I was out of my bed and rushing down the hall to Quentin's room. As quickly as I moved though, Mrs. Barclay was there before me. When I entered Quentin's bedroom, she was crouched beside the bed, cradling the sobbing figure in her arms, crooning softly, "There, there, my sweet. Don't be afraid. I won't let the cavalier hurt you."

I had noticed that a small night light was always kept burning in Quentin's room. Now I turned the lamp higher and asked, "What happened? Is he ill?"

Quentin lifted his face, glistening white and tear stained, to stare accusingly at me. "It wasn't the cavalier. It was the headless horseman. He was chasing me."

So that was it, I thought relieved. Only a nightmare. I smiled coaxingly at the boy. "It was just a funny story, Quentin. The headless horseman wasn't really a ghost."

"What's going on?" Jason appeared in the doorway, Rowena behind him, blinking sleepily.

Charlotte Barclay's voice throbbed with anger. "Miss Prentice has been telling Quentin ghost stories. The child had one of his nightmares."

I gazed bewildered from the woman's anger to Jason's face that was beginning to cloud with annoyance as he frowned at me. "Couldn't you find something more suitable to read to the boy, Miss Prentice? Anyway, I thought you were supposed to teach Quentin to read, not waste time telling him stories."

I bit back the furious retort that sprang to my lips. How could I explain that Quentin was too spoiled, too indolent to put forth the effort to learn to read. I had thought by reading stories aloud to him that he might, in time, become interested enough to want to learn to read the stories himself.

"I'm sorry, Mr. Barclay," I said stiffly. "Perhaps you should make other arrangements for a tutor."

I caught the fleeting look of triumph on Charlotte Barclay's face before I turned and marched back to my room. I had almost reached the door of the blue bedroom when a hand grasped my shoulder and turned me around to face my sheepish-looking employer. "I spoke too sharply, Miss Prentice. Earlier this evening and now, too. My manners, I'm afraid, are not as courteous as they should be with young ladies. I hope you'll reconsider and stay on."

I stood silent, uncertain. I knew I had spoken impulsively, through wounded pride. I needed this job here at Fernwood. And yet, how could I teach Quentin successfully when from the beginning there had been an undercurrent of resistance toward all my efforts.

"Has Quentin had these nightmares for long?" I asked slowly.

Jason hesitated a moment, then nodded. "For several years now. When he was little he used to get out of bed and roam around the house at night. One of the servants, without our knowledge, told the boy the story about the ghostly cavalier that's supposed to haunt Fernwood, to frighten the boy into staying in his room at night. By the time we found out, the damage was done. Now Quentin seems convinced that some sort of spectral apparition walks the halls of Fernwood at night."

"Has Quentin ever . . . ever seen this cavalier?"

"Of course not!" Jason scowled. "How could the boy possibly see something that doesn't exist?"

But I had taught school too long not to sense when I was being lied to, and I felt a surge of irritation. How could I cope with Quentin if I weren't told the whole story behind his fears? And the truth was, even if I didn't need the job, I didn't want to give up teaching him. For all my pupil's lack of discipline, his childish arrogance, I had grown fond of the boy. Occasionally I had glimpsed in those pale blue eyes fastened upon me, a forlorn, desperate fear, demanding something of me, what I didn't know.

"Very well, Mr. Barclay. If you want me to, I'll continue working as Quentin's tutor."

As it turned out, however, I had no choice in the matter. The next morning when I came down to breakfast I discovered that Jason Barclay had left early that morning for Richmond, "a business trip" Rowena said shortly, and that Mrs. Charlotte had sent word to me that Quentin wasn't well enough for lessons, and she was keeping the boy in his room for a few days.

With no lessons to give, time hung heavy on my hands. I no longer walked out to the tobacco fields. It had been interesting when I might catch a glimpse of Jason Barclay in the fields and have a chance to talk with him about the progress of the tobacco crop, but now there would only be Giles, and I certainly had no desire to talk to him.

In order to have some exercise, I began walking through the gardens of Fernwood. These walks, however, were always more a determined trek than a leisurely stroll. Shrub roses, lilacs, Carolina all spice, spirea, unpruned for too many years, made a jungle out of what had once been carefully tended paths. Despite all the obstacles, though, I thought I had managed to ex-

plore most of the garden until the third morning. I was following a curved, yew-lined path when I came to an abrupt dead
end. Retracing my steps, puzzled, I noticed a break in what I
had thought was a solid wall of yew. Pushing aside the branches,
I stepped through the narrow opening. Then gazed around me
in startled delight.

I was in an ivy-carpeted cul-de-sac surrounded by towering
azaleas and walls of mock orange. A dogwood tree made a
webbed, lacy roof over my head through which sunlight filtered,
washing the small garden with a luminous green glow. In the
center of this square of verdant growth, as if drifting on an
emerald sea, floated the pillars of a dainty white summerhouse.

At least, the gazebo had once been white. The paint had almost disappeared from the pillars and the grilled iron dome
was disfigured with rust, but the innate fragile beauty of the
building could still be seen.

As I stepped closer, I was aware of a deep somnolence lying
like a spell over the garden. The eerie feeling possessed me that
I was the first person to have entered this portion of the garden
or gazed upon the whimsical little summerhouse in years.

I sat down to rest on the summerhouse steps, a heaviness
tugging at my heart. Of the many deserted ruins I had seen in
the South, this forsaken gazebo seemed the most pathetic. As if
all these years it had been standing, patiently waiting for the
return of its lovely ladies and gallant gentlemen, the whispers
and laughter, the stolen kisses and romantic tête-à-têtes. And
Celia, I thought. Had she visited here, rested on pillows in this
shadowy green light, with Jason beside her, making plans,
dreaming of a future that would never be . . .

Abruptly I got to my feet, shaking off the depression that lay
like a black shawl around my shoulders. I was being fanciful.
How did I know Celia had even seen the little summerhouse? I
was bored, that's all, I decided. I wasn't used to idleness or I
wouldn't be spending so much time morbidly thinking about
Celia Rougier, trying to imagine how she felt, what she had
been like.

At dinner that day I approached Rowena with an idea that

had come to me as I wandered through Fernwood's neglected gardens. "Do you think anyone would mind, while Quentin isn't well, if I did some gardening?"

Rowena looked surprised. "I suppose not but I'm afraid you'll find it an impossible task. Uncle Guy always had three gardeners and even they couldn't keep up with the work."

"Oh, I wouldn't try and work on the whole garden at once," I explained. "I thought perhaps I'd start with that little garden by the gazebo. It would be a wonderful place for afternoon teas, that is, if the summerhouse could be repaired. Is it very old?"

"No, not old at all," Rowena said, her voice oddly strained. "The summerhouse was built the first week Celia came to Fernwood. In fact, that part of the garden was planned especially for her by Uncle Guy as a wedding present. All the flowers and shrubs were to be white, Celia's favorite color. Not that she ever saw any of them in bloom. Guy ordered the roses and azaleas for the garden from New Orleans. They arrived the day before she died."

She lowered her eyes, watching me through the sparse gold lashes. "You won't get any servants to help you with the gardening, you know. They're all convinced the summerhouse is haunted. Jonas even claims he saw the cavalier one night in the garden." Rowena's nose twitched disapprovingly. "No doubt he'd been at the cooking sherry." She got to her feet and headed for the door, tossing back over her shoulder, "By the way, Cousin Robert sent word he's paying us a visit. He should be here this evening sometime . . ."

Despite Rowena's pessimism, I determined to go ahead with my gardening plans. At least it would give me something to do. Then as I returned to my room that evening, I remembered the gardening journals I had seen in the library the first morning I toured Fernwood Hall. Perhaps they would help me in my renovation work in Celia's garden.

Bed could wait, I decided, and, taking my lamp, went quickly down the stairs into the library. As I entered the room, a curtain by a partly opened window stirred, as if from a fitful breeze. It had been an unusually hot, humid day and I hoped the breeze was bringing rain to cool the air. After several minutes, I located the gardening ledgers. As I removed them, the dust rising from their covers made me sneeze.

My sneeze seemed to mingle with another, softer sound in the room, a shuffling, muffled noise. Putting down the books, I raised my lamp higher. I could swear the curtain at the window was still swaying although the breeze had fallen away. Then I heard it again, no louder than a breath. I strained my eyes through the darkness but I could see no one. Yet I knew. I was not alone in the library.

CHAPTER NINE

My hand trembled but I kept a tight hold on the lamp. "Who's there?" I demanded. I saw the curtains stir again. I raised the lamp higher so that the circle of light spread protectively around me.

"Come out at once," I ordered, "or I'll call for help."

A shadow moved, separated from the dark, and stepped forward.

"Si!" I lowered the lamp with a sigh of relief. "For heaven's sake, what are you doing here this time of night?"

The young, frightened mouth quivered, the eyes on the verge of tears. I placed the lamp on the desk and said soothingly, "It's all right, Si. I'm not angry." I saw the book he clutched in his hand and asked, shocked, "You weren't stealing books from the library?"

"No'm, I ain't no thief. I jes sneaks in at night with a candle when everyone's sleepin' and I read. I don't hurt the books none."

I glanced at the title of the book he held. *Ivanhoe* by Walter Scott. I smiled in disbelief. "Surely you aren't able to read that."

"Not all the words," he admitted. "Some I can figure out after a time . . . I listened real careful to Marse Quentin's teachers." A look of frustration twisted the young face. "Some words though, the letters wiggle away and make no sense at all."

I stood, without speaking, imagining how it must have been for the boy, struggling to understand the strange scratchings on the page as if through sheer force of will alone. How intently he must have been listening while I taught the reading lessons to Quentin and I hadn't even noticed. Abruptly I went to the bookcase and selected a dog-eared copy of a child's primer. "Here, this will be easier for you. You can take it with you."

His eyes watched me warily and I assured him, "It's all right. I'll explain to your grandmother how you got the book. And if you like, I'll help you with the words you don't understand."

If only there were some way the boy could spend some time with me, so I could work with him each day. I gazed thoughtfully at Si. "Now that Quentin isn't feeling well enough for lessons, I thought I'd try my hand at gardening, the little garden near the summerhouse. Would you like to help me and I'll help you with your reading."

The boy's eyes widened, his hand tightening on the book. "Miss Celia's garden? Nothing grows there but poison plants and hants."

So Si was afraid of the garden, too. I suppose I should have expected that. I smiled to hide my disappointment. "Never mind, Si. Now you'd better run along before Dulcy misses you."

He turned to the window, hesitated, then spun around, speaking in a rush. "You teach me to read, Miss Abigail. I'll help with your gardening." Then he scrambled out of the window.

I closed the window after him against the first scattered raindrops. Lightning flickered across the treetops, illuminating the tiny figure dashing across the lawn to the cabin where he lived with Dulcy and Jonas.

Picking up the lamp and several of the gardening books, I left the library, then paused a moment outside the closed doors of the drawing room. Obeying a sudden impulse, I placed the books on the entrance table and went inside. My lamp moved past the faces of Barclay ancestors, bringing them to momentary life then plunging them into darkness again. Finally I stopped before the portrait of Charlotte Barclay's husband, Guy. With his heavy jowls, his rather pompous expression, I somehow wouldn't have thought him capable of designing the exquisite little summerhouse, the hidden garden. In any case, it seemed an unusual present for a man to make to his sister-in-law-to-be. I was wondering what Charlotte had thought about the gift when I heard the door slam in the front hall and footsteps above the sound of the rising wind and rain.

The footsteps stopped outside the drawing-room door, then after a moment, advanced into the room. I turned guiltily, clutching the lamp.

"Miss Prentice?" Robert Barclay's voice sounded surprised, as if for the first time I had caught him off guard. "What are you doing down here at this time of night?"

As he strode toward me, I could see the rain glistening in his silver-blond hair, the amused curiosity in the gray-blue eyes. I devoutly wished now that I had gone straight back to my bedroom without making this detour to look at Guy Barclay's portrait.

"I . . . I was borrowing some reading material from the library . . . your brother's gardening journals." I heard myself stammering, the way I always do when I'm ill at ease.

Rob's eyebrow lifted quizzically at my choice of reading material, and I hastened on, more firmly. "I saw the summerhouse today for the first time. Rowena told me your brother Guy built it for Miss Rougier. Such a lovely gift. It must have pleased her greatly."

My companion's mouth twisted into a rueful smile. "Dear Celia," he murmured. "We all tried to please her, each in his own way."

At my expression, he grinned boyishly. "No, I wasn't immune to her charms either. And they were considerable. But I was the youngest brother and she had bigger fish to fry."

"You sound . . . as if you disliked her."

Rob looked startled, then laughed. "Toward a woman like Celia, a man seldom had such lukewarm feelings as like or dislike. For a few days she even had me believing . . . but then, our Celia had a way of making each man feel as if he, alone, mattered." His voice grew grim. "Only with Jason, she picked a dangerous man to play that game. I remember an evening a few weeks before the wedding when I was walking in the garden with Jason. Unfortunately, there was a particularly bright moon that night. It was impossible not to see Brian and Celia together in the summerhouse. Jason turned away without saying a word but I saw his face. I'm not likely to ever forget the look I saw there."

"What are you saying?" I demanded indignantly. "After all, it was Brian who . . ."

"Who killed her," Robert Barclay finished my sentence for me when I fell silent, embarrassed.

"I'm sorry. I shouldn't have . . ."

Before I could finish, Rob snatched the lamp from my hand. His fingers tightened cruelly on my arm, turning me to face the portrait of Brian Barclay. The lamplight touched the laughing mouth, the careless amusement in the eyes. Rob's voice rasped in my ear: "Tell me, is that the face of a murderer, a man who would lift his hand against a woman?"

"But he ran away! Why did he run then? Or when he heard what had happened, why didn't he come back and clear himself?"

Rob stared at his brother's portrait without speaking for several moments, as if trying to find an answer there. "I've thought about it often enough," he said slowly. "I've even thought he might have been protecting someone. It's the sort of quixotic gesture Brian would make, not stopping to think what it would cost him. In spite of their difference, he was fond of Jason, you know. Even though he did tease him a lot. Until Jason turned on him one day and almost killed him."

At my cry of protest, he shrugged. "It was just boys fighting, but it got out of hand. Jason lost his head. He always was strong as an ox. Luckily Giles was near and pulled Jason off in time. After that, Uncle Guy decided it was best to separate them. Jason was sent off to a boy's school and then went on to the University of Virginia. Brian and he didn't see much of each other again until Jason came back from Paris with Celia." Rob turned to me, his voice thoughtful. "I've often wondered, suppose at the last minute Celia changed her mind. Women do, you know. What if she decided it was Brian she wanted, after all, and Jason found out."

"Jason was at Silver Grove!"

"He could have left without anybody knowing. I wouldn't have noticed. A bachelor party isn't noted for its sobriety and I'm afraid the drinks got the better of me early in the festivities."

"Are you accusing your brother of murder?" I asked, shocked.

He shrugged. "It's an interesting possibility. And Jason's always hated giving up anything he thought belonged to him."

Instead of returning the lamp to me, he set it down on the table beside him. I watched him, suddenly uneasy. At our first meeting, Robert Barclay had treated me with an indifferent politeness, his glance skimming over me, not really seeing me. There was nothing casual about his gaze now, the way it lingered on my face, traveled down my body.

"You know," he drawled, "for a moment when I walked in here tonight, I thought you were Celia."

I must have shown the disbelief I felt, for he shook his head. "No, not your face. She didn't have that gypsy slant to the eyes or the prim expression your mouth wears. And her skin was velvet white as a camellia, not tawny like yours. But the way you hold your head is the same and the lovely way you fill out that gown." He grinned teasingly. "Now, have I finally shocked you, Miss Prim and Proper Abigail? There's one more thing you have in common with Celia, your hair—masses of soft darkness. Only Celia never bound her hair. She always wore it loose, so a man could bury his face in it, breathe her perfume—"

Before I could stop him, before I even knew what he was about, his hands reached behind me and expertly removed the two hairpins that bound my chignon. I felt my hair fall slowly around my shoulders, prickling my skin, or perhaps it was the warmth I suddenly felt that made my skin tighten. Then before I could move, Robert's mouth came down upon mine, tenderly at first, a feather lightly brushing my lips then with a growing urgency. For a moment I felt myself responding, as if some hunger deep inside of me was answering his. For a moment only. Then I thrust him away, furious with him and even angrier with myself.

He laughed softly. "I suppose I should say I'm sorry, Abigail, but it'd be a lie. And I don't think you're sorry either. A man can always tell."

My palm itched to slap that smug look from his handsome face but in a way, that would be a triumph for him, too. I contented myself in snatching up my lamp and stalking away, aware that he was following me quietly.

At the stairs, his voice stopped me. "Wait, you're forgetting your journals." He handed the ledgers to me, smiling confidently. "I thought tomorrow we could go riding together. I could show you something of the countryside around Fernwood. It must be deadly dull for you around here."

"I'm going to be busy tomorrow," I said flatly, and was pleased at the look of surprise flitting momentarily across Robert Barclay's face, before I turned away and climbed the stairs to my room.

Yet, once in my room, I found myself stopping, gazing curiously into the dressing table mirror. Why, I was almost pretty, I thought surprised. The sun had dusted my skin with gold and Cindy's cooking had put back the weight I had lost after father's death. My dress no longer hung loose on my frame but fit snugly across the bodice. The gaunt, hollow look of grief was vanished and with my hair hanging dark and loose to my shoulders, my face seemed softer, my cheeks flushed with pink, my eyes glowing. Did I really resemble Celia?

The thought came, unbidden, and I quickly thrust it away. I wasn't some naïve servant girl that Robert Barclay could flatter and amuse himself with, stealing kisses in dark corners. Nevertheless, as I undressed and climbed into bed, I faced the uncomfortable truth that I had enjoyed that kiss. And the even more humiliating fact that for all my advanced years, it was the first time any man had ever kissed me. Not that it had mattered to me before.

I had been too busy attending college, then teaching and keeping house for my father to waste my time, indulging in girlish flirtations. And the occasional men I had brought home after a few minutes' conversation with my father, I quickly saw

how dull and uninteresting they were. They never returned a
second time.

I shifted restlessly in my bed. The wind had risen, bringing
more rain from the west, tapping lightly at the window. I got
up to stand a moment at the open window. My face felt flushed
and I reached out my hands, caught the soft rain in my palms
and ran my hands over my face, cooling my skin . . . suddenly
remembering a ballad I had read years before and never forgotten.

> O Western wind, when wilt thou blow
> That the small rain down can rain?
> Christ, that my love were in my arms,
> And I in my bed again!

What would it be like to feel passion like that, I wondered,
an odd ache pressing just beneath my breastbone. Not only to
be kissed but to lie in bed in a man's arms. Celia must have
known . . .

Then hastily I closed the window, turned up the lamp and determinedly reached for one of the gardening journals. If I was
going to stay awake, I might as well use the time profitably. I
soon discovered that the gardening journals were certainly dull
enough to act as a soporific. Most of the entries were brief nota-
tions about the weather, routine work in the garden, planting
and weeding and insect blights noted.

Finally I came across several drawings which I instantly recognized, the small gazebo with its filigreed roof, and the names
of the shrubs and flowers to be planted around the summerhouse. The next pages were filled with Guy's notes about the
garden. The summerhouse was completed quickly but aggravat-
ingly, the azaleas and roses specially ordered were late in arriving. A dogwood of the proper size and shape had been found
in the woods and replanted in the garden, the mock orange and
yew hedge installed. Then, on April 3, the notation that the
azaleas and roses had finally arrived. And there the journal
ended. After that, blank pages.

Suddenly I realized why. April 4 must have been the morning

Celia was found, shot to death in her room. Naturally Guy wouldn't have felt like continuing the journal. Evidently, after Celia's death, he had never written in the journal again.

Frustrated, I closed the book and turned out the lamp. Well, at least, I knew now how the garden should look. Si and I could make a start, weeding and pruning. If nothing else, I told myself, the gardening activity would give me an excuse to keep out of Robert Barclay's way.

For the next few days Si and I worked steadily in the small garden. When the sun became too hot to work, we'd stop and sit on the gazebo steps, and I'd listen to Si read aloud, helping him when he stumbled but surprised at how quickly his mind grasped what I taught him. After Quentin's obdurate refusal to even try to learn, Si's eagerness to absorb everything was a constant joy.

And my gardening work did keep me away from Robert Barclay. Sometimes though in the evening when we sat together in the sitting room with the French door open to catch the breeze, always with Miss Rowena or Mrs. Charlotte for chaperones, I would feel his eyes on me, catch an amused look on his face, and I had the feeling that he knew exactly what I was doing. That he was simply waiting for the inevitable moment when I could no longer avoid him.

And then the third morning something happened which momentarily drove all thoughts of Robert Barclay from my mind. Si and I were digging up several azalea bushes that had died when suddenly he called out to me, "Miss Abigail, come see what I found."

I had been studying the summerhouse, wondering if paint would be enough to refurbish it or if the wood were rotten and would need shoring up. Absently I walked over to where Si was kneeling. He held up to me a clump of dirt brought up from the hole left by the azalea bush, tossed to one side. At first, I thought it an oddly formed rock. Then Si broke off bits of earth around the object and it began to take shape. And finally I recognized it for what it was, or rather what it had been. A gun.

CHAPTER TEN

I took the gun from Si's hand. The metal barrel was rusted and clogged with dirt, the wooden stock rotted. As I rubbed away more of the dirt, I could see where there was some sort of fancy silver inlay decoration on the stock.

"How do you reckon a gun got buried here, Miss Abigail?"

"I haven't any idea, Si. Perhaps during the war, when soldiers were quartered here at Fernwood."

"Can I keep it?" Si asked eagerly.

"It may belong to someone at the hall. Why don't you see how well you can clean it up and I'll ask Mr. Barclay about it."

I turned my attention back to the problem of the summerhouse, wondering again if it could be repaired. The next morning at breakfast I brought up the subject. Rob shrugged indifferently. "You'd better ask Giles. He was the one who was in charge of the construction. In my opinion, though, it's probably termite eaten and should be torn down."

"It's the focal point of the garden," I protested.

Mrs. Barclay's alabaster cheeks grew pink. "The idea of the gazebo was completely impractical from the beginning. I told Mr. Barclay so myself."

She stopped speaking when Dulcy came into the room, carrying a bright red kerchief. "Si brought this to the kitchen, Miss Prentice," she said, handing the bundle to me, a look of grim disapproval on her face. "Why you giving that boy of mine a gun, Miss Prentice?"

"What's this about a gun?" Rob got to his feet and came around the table as I unwrapped the kerchief.

"Si found it in the garden by the summerhouse," I explained. The boy had done a good job of cleaning the weapon. The wooden stock was beyond repair but the silver inlay had been polished till you could see clearly the pattern traced in the silver, a group of fern fronds intertwined.

Rob picked up the gun, studying it. Charlotte Barclay's white hands grasped the edge of the table, as if to steady herself. Her voice was low. "Is it . . ." She couldn't seem to finish.

Rob nodded, giving his sister-in-law an oddly covert glance. "It's the mate all right, Charlotte. You can still see the name of the gunsmith on the lock, C. Bird & Co."

"The mate to what?" I asked, bewildered. Rob left the room without a word and returned with a handsome carved mahogany case. When he lifted the lid, I could see tucked into one section of the red velvet lining a highly polished dueling pistol. The ten-inch-long barrel and walnut stock gleamed; the delicately etched silver fern inlay matched exactly the gun Si had found. My hand reached to touch the gun then drew back quickly, all at once understanding. This must be the gun that killed Celia Rougier.

"The dueling pistols were originally flintlocks," Rob said to me. "They were converted to percussion when flintlocks became obsolete. Brian always kept them in his room . . ."

I gestured to the case. "Where was this . . . gun found?"

"In Celia's hand," Rowena answered for Rob. "The mate was missing from the case. Everyone assumed Brian took it with him after . . ." she broke off, flushing.

Charlotte Barclay's arm went protectively around young Quentin who was listening, silent and wide-eyed to the conversation. "The breakfast table is hardly the time and place for a discussion like this," she said coldly. "Please take that pistol away at once, Robert. You know how I feel about guns."

"But it's mine," Quentin protested, twisting from his aunt's grasp. "The pistols belonged to my father so they're mine now, aren't they?"

The look of anguish on Charlotte Barclay's face ripped away her usual cool composure, her icy grande-dame manner.

Robert thrust the guns into the red velvet case and closed it quickly, giving Quentin a winning smile. "How would you like to go riding with me this morning, Quent? We could go over to Wilson's woods. I saw a fox burrow there yesterday."

"Could I? Could we go right away?" Quentin's eyes danced with excitement. He adored his dashing Uncle Rob and tagged after him whenever he could.

"Right now," Rob promised, leaving the room with Quentin trailing happily after him. I was glad to see the guns leave. They had brought something dark and ugly into the pleasant dining room, the smell of death and decay.

Dulcy began to gather up the breakfast dishes, mumbling under her breath, "I told Jonas no good would come of my Si digging 'round that garden."

"That's enough, Dulcy," Rowena snapped. "Don't forget to take Mr. Giles his breakfast. He sent word he isn't feeling well."

Once Rowena and Mrs. Barclay were safely out of the room, Dulcy continued her grumbling. "Upsetting Mrs. Charlotte that way, bringing that gun in here . . ."

"I'm sorry, Dulcy," I apologized. "It was my fault. I didn't realize firearms bothered Mrs. Barclay."

"How do you 'spect her to feel?" Dulcy asked belligerently. "During the war, Mrs. Charlotte seen her own father shot down before her eyes. Ever since, she can't bear to look at a gun, turns her stomach to touch one. I should be with Mrs. Charlotte now, 'stead of toting food to that no count Giles . . ."

I got to my feet and offered, "I'll take Mr. Latham's tray to him. I want to talk to him anyway about the summerhouse."

Dulcy was only too happy to be relieved of the task. Tray in hand I mounted the narrow staircase that led to Giles's living quarters above the stable. Outside the door, I took a deep breath, gathered my courage, and knocked.

I heard a muffled command to come in and I pushed open the door. I'm not sure what I expected, probably an ill-kept bachelor's quarters. Although now that I thought about it, I remembered Dulcy had once mentioned that Giles had been married in New Orleans at one time but that his wife had run off and left him, which action on her part, I reflected grimly, I could certainly understand.

"Come in or go out," the man growled from a large chair by the window. "Don't stand there, gawking." Spotting the tray I carried, he grimaced in what passed for a smile. "So it's mistress of the house you're playing at this morning."

I walked across the room, placed the tray beside the chair. I will never forget the smell of the man, the odor of tobacco, cheap whiskey and the stale smell of clothes that need a good airing.

"Miss Rowena is busy."

He snorted contemptuously. "Aye, busy, tending someone else's home, living on the Barclay leavings. If she had any sense, she'd have a home of her own by now and a man's bed to warm."

I saw the milky eyes watching me beneath hooded lids, testing me, using his coarseness deliberately to send me scurrying off like a scared mouse.

I held my breath against the stench and refused to back away, my voice tart, "You wouldn't have the nerve to say that in front of Jason Barclay."

For a moment something akin to grudging respect crept into his eyes and his gaze dropped. "That I wouldn't," he admitted. "When she first came to Fernwood, I made a fair and honorable offer for the woman, almost got thrashed by old Guy for my pains. I learned my lesson and I've not forgot. Giles Latham may be dirt for the Barclays to walk on but he's no man's fool to make the same mistake twice."

I sat down on a straight-back chair, stifling a hysterical feeling of amusement as I imagined that scene, Giles asking for Rowena's hand in marriage. With the Barclays' highly refined sense of family, I could imagine the reception that proposal got!

"If you dislike the Barclays so much, I'm surprised you've continued working for them all these years."

He gave me a glance of mocking innocence. "Now why should I dislike fine people like the Barclays? It's a pleasure and honor to work for them. I admire to watch their quality airs, the way they hold their heads so high like they were better than everything and everybody on God's green earth. It's been an education for a poor, simple man like myself."

"You could have left." There was something evil about the mocking servility, at the hatred that simmered beneath the surface of that voice. "Why didn't you leave Fernwood, go work somewhere else?"

"Leave!" A brick red flowed beneath the rough, tanned skin; the hands clenching into horny fists on the arms of the chair. "Why should I leave? Fernwood belongs to me, as much as to the Barclays, aye, more. Do you think that land belongs to a man because of a piece of paper with writing on it? No! The land belongs to the man who works it, cherishes it, tends it with his blood and sweat. It's my sweat for the last forty years that's watered the soil of Fernwood while the Barclays sat back in their parlor, playing at being gentlemen. It's me that tricked the Yankees out of burning Fernwood to the ground. It's my hands that whipped the slaves to work at the tobacco till they dropped, while the Barclays' conscience, not seeing or hearing their screams, could remain pure as snow."

Suddenly he thrust his hands toward me and I saw, shocked, that every nail was stained an indelible green. "It's the tobacco on them that never rubs off. It's these hands that fought the drought and the pests all by themselves during the war years to save the land, and after the war, kept on working while money was thrown away on fancy furniture and fine geegaws for the mansion there. It's these hands . . ."

He stopped short, gazing at me with a blurred bewilderment, as if recalling himself with a physical wrench back to the present and my face, staring at him, speechless. He took a deep, hoarse breath and once again that grimace of a smile appeared and he gestured around him. "Now why should I leave all my dear things, all the home I've ever known?"

As my eyes had grown accustomed to the gloom, I had noticed that the large room, for all it could use a good airing, was comfortably, even handsomely furnished.

The man poked at the food I had brought, muttering irritably. "Gruel and toast. Do they think I'm dying? How can a man gain back his strength on the likes of this? With Jason away, I should be up and about."

"The tobacco's doing fine," I assured him. "You can see for yourself."

As, indeed, he could. His window looked out across the thriving tobacco fields, changed from an emerald green to a yellowish-green, the huge leaves shirred like silk at the edges.

I said soothingly, "I understand Mr. Barclay is away on business. I'm sure it's important or he wouldn't have gone."

"Business, is it? It's money he's after, no doubt. The way that fool Guy threw away good cash on the hall like water down a drain, and young Robert no better with his gambling and wenching. It's a wonder there's any money left. A good marriage, I told Jason, that's what was needed. A rich wife he should find himself the way Guy did." He chuckled in his throat. "Though it's young Rob who has the Barclay eye for the ladies."

"The private affairs of the Barclay family are no concern of mine or yours either," I said coldly.

Giles nodded, unperturbed. "Aye, that's true enough." He took a last gulp of coffee and gave me a sharp glance. "And now what was it you wanted? It wasn't to bring a sick old man his breakfast, I'm thinking."

Swallowing my pride, I said, "I did want some information about the little summerhouse in the garden."

When he stared at me blankly, without speaking, I continued impatiently, "You must know what I mean, the gazebo that Mr. Guy Barclay had constructed as a wedding present for Miss Rougier."

"I know it." He was silent a long moment. When he spoke again, his voice was peevish, "And who gave you permission to interfere in the gardens?"

"I'm not interfering. I'm simply trying to refurbish the little garden around the summerhouse."

"And a silly notion it was," he grumbled. "I built the foolish thing according to Mr. Guy's drawings and a blasphemous waste of good lumber it was, too. Not to speak of all those fancy plants

Mr. Guy had to have for the garden, sent up specially from New Orleans. Then when she went and got herself killed, it was me that had the work of finishing the planting. Not that I noticed any of the Barclays had the stomach to come look at the garden or her fancy summerhouse afterward. Not one of them that she made fools of with her high and mighty manners and all the time common as dirt she was underneath."

The last seemed to explode from the man in a vitriolic explosion that would have repelled me if I hadn't been fascinated by what the man was revealing about Celia Rougier.

"Did you know her well?"

"Well!" He laughed, a sharp, ugly sound. "I knew her type well, for all her fine airs. A Rampart Street floozy was what I first thought."

Rampart Street, I thought confused. That was in New Orleans, wasn't it? "You mean she wasn't French?" I asked, surprised.

"She spoke the language like a frogsticker well enough," he admitted. "With a voice like honey in her mouth. A pretty piece of goods she was with those big black eyes and that white skin. And the way she had of moving her body so a man knew just what she was offering him, any man. Jason was lucky to be rid of her. He should have found himself a decent woman with a good inheritance and counted himself fortunate."

"And Brian? What of Brian Barclay and Celia?" I couldn't resist asking.

Giles's face filled with a gloating malice. "Aye, and he was the biggest fool of them all. It was comical to watch, him that had his way with so many women, charm oozing out of him like sweat from other men, getting hooked himself good and proper. I've often wondered at the end how he felt, knowing her for what she was, what a fool she'd made of him."

"Do you think that's why . . . why he killed her, because he found out she wasn't what she seemed?"

Giles shrugged his massive shoulders; his eyes hooded, his voice indifferent. "Now how should I be knowing what a man's thinking when he takes a pistol and shoots a woman? Let the dead be buried and forgotten, I say."

I stared at the man, suddenly sensed the truth. Giles didn't think Brian killed Celia either. "It had to be Brian," I blurted. "They were his guns and now that we've found the second one in the garden . . ."

Giles jerked forward. I thought he was going to grab my arm and I shrank back at the thought of those green hands touching me. "What are you gabbing about? What gun?"

I told him about the mate to the dueling pistol that Si had found. When I had finished talking, he glared at me. "An able-bodied boy like Si shouldn't be playing around in the garden. And if you have any sense at all, you'll forget this foolishness with the summerhouse and stop meddling in matters that are none of your concern."

Once more his eyes clashed with mine, but this time it was my gaze that fell away, frightened at the implacable hatred in the man's face. Anyway he was right, I thought unhappily. I had been brought to Fernwood to teach Quentin, not to pry into old family scandals. Celia's death was none of my concern. And yet . . . I saw Quentin's face, the way he had looked that day on the road to the tobacco field, the sad, hunched shoulders, the stricken look in his eyes whenever his father's name was mentioned. "Don't you see?" I pleaded. "If Brian Barclay didn't kill the woman, it isn't fair Quentin should go through life, believing his father a murderer."

Giles turned his face away from me, mumbling almost to himself. "I should have known you'd have a long, prying Yankee nose." A lascivious smile suddenly licked at his lips. "You'd best be careful though before you poke it into more than you bargained for."

"What do you mean?"

He chuckled deep in his throat. "And don't you think I've noticed the way your eyes follow Jason Barclay around like a puppy dog, making excuses to come out to the fields to talk to him, swinging your skirt so he'll notice you. A man who's killed once develops a taste for it. You think he'll stop at a second time?"

I sprang to my feet, too angry to be afraid. "Are you accusing

Mr. Jason Barclay of murdering the French girl?" I asked coldly. "If so, I'm sure Mr. Barclay would be most interested to hear of it."

"You'll not tell Jason anything," he said calmly. "Or he'll be wanting to know why you were pestering me with questions about him and the girl. If you know Jason at all, you'll know he won't thank you for digging at old graves."

"We'll see about that," I said, turning and sweeping furiously from the room. But as I hurried down the narrow staircase, clinging for support to the rough, wooden balustrade, I knew Giles was right about one thing.

I wouldn't tell Jason Barclay about our conversation.

CHAPTER ELEVEN

Later that afternoon as I worked in Celia's garden, yanking out weeds as if they were my mortal enemy, it was not the weeds I saw. It was Giles's shrewdly knowing face, taunting me, as he huddled in his chair by the window like a spider in the center of his web. I was sure now that he knew more about Celia's death than he had ever told. Except, I frowned and sank back on my heels, Giles hadn't been at Fernwood the night Celia died. Rowena told me he had returned the next morning.

Still, there was only Giles's word for that. Suppose he lied. Suppose he had returned to Fernwood earlier than he claimed and found all the men gone to the party at Silver Grove and Celia left alone and unprotected. If he had made advances and the girl threatened to tell Jason . . . no, that wouldn't do. He would hardly have forced his way into Celia's bedroom, and how would he have gained possession of the dueling pistols. In any case, I couldn't imagine Giles using those pistols with which to kill. Oh, I could see those thorny, green-tipped hands strangling or beating a woman to death in a fit of rage, but . . .

"Miss Abigail." Si spoke timidly behind me. "Those ain't weeds you're pulling. That's the white phlox you asked me to plant."

Guiltily I glanced down at the ground and saw the torn up plants lying wilted and dying all around me. "I'm sorry, Si." Penitently I tried to press the torn-up roots back into the ground. "Maybe we should stop for the day. It's almost too warm for working."

"Yes'm," and then wistfully, "you think maybe soon Marse Quentin will be able to play with me again?"

"I hope so, Si," I said, smiling encouragingly.

At least, that evening Mrs. Charlotte allowed Quentin to join us for supper. The boy seemed listless and Charlotte kept coaxing him to eat. It was a hot evening and I barely toyed with my food myself.

Rowena, noticing, asked if I weren't feeling well.

"It's just the heat," I said, pushing aside my plate. "Too much sun this afternoon, I expect."

Mrs. Charlotte cocked her head birdlike to one side, studying my face. "I hope you won't take offense, my dear, but you really should remember to wear a hat when you're outdoors." She laughed prettily. "I suppose I'm old-fashioned but in my day you could always tell a lady by her complexion. If you'd like, I have a face cream you can borrow. It's from a recipe of my mother's. It does wonders to keep your skin soft and white. It'd be a shame for Jason to come home and find you brown as a field hand."

Rowena said quickly, "You shouldn't work so hard in the garden, Abigail."

"I don't mind," I said, refusing to rise to Mrs. Barclay's bait. But inwardly I winced. First, Giles, now Mrs. Barclay. Was it so obvious then, my feelings about Jason? "I enjoy working outdoors. And Si does most of the heavy jobs."

"Speaking of Si . . ." Mrs. Barclay took the conversational reins firmly back in her hand . . . "I saw that he had a book from the library the other day. He said you had given him permission to borrow it."

"Yes, I did. I hope you don't mind. He's very careful with books."

"But isn't it a waste of time? I mean, the boy can't possibly read them."

"Yes, he can," I said eagerly, forgetting caution in pride in my pupil. "It's amazing how quickly he's learning."

I broke off, dismayed. A hardness settled like frost over Mrs. Barclay's face. Then she said, very gently, "Naturally, you wouldn't be expected to understand, Miss Prentice, not being born and reared in the South, but teaching the Negro to read and write, well, it's simply not wise. Before the war, it was even against the law. When a black boy starts getting learning, he only ends up in trouble. Now I think the world and all of Dulcy, but she'd be the first to be unhappy about what you're doing to Si."

That's not true, I thought indignantly. Dulcy was proud of Si's ability to read. I had seen the pride in her eyes the morning Si had shown her that he could read a whole page of a book straight through.

Mrs. Charlotte shivered delicately. "I'd hate to think what our neighbors in the county would say if they heard we were conducting a school for Negro students here at Fernwood Hall!"

"It's hardly a school," I pointed out. "It's only one boy."

Mrs. Barclay eyed me imperiously. Was I really insisting upon defying her? "Nevertheless, I'm sure Jason would never approve. After all, you were employed to teach Quentin, you may recall, not the servants' children."

And I can't even do that, I thought, as long as you won't allow Quentin to attend classes. This time, however, I was determined not to back down. I clasped my hands beneath the table so she could not see their trembling and made my voice as composed as possible. "Perhaps we should wait till Mr. Barclay returns and let him decide."

I heard Rowena draw in her breath, a sharp gasp of alarm. Mrs. Barclay got to her feet, her eyes watching me glittered with fury. "Very well, we'll let Mr. Barclay decide. Come along, Quentin."

The boy got slowly to his feet, giving me a speculative glance, then shrugged and followed his aunt out of the room. I half suspected he was sorry he wasn't taking lessons from me any longer but had too much pride to admit it. Surely it must be boring for a boy Quentin's age to be kept so closely tucked under his aunt's wing.

Rowena scuttled after them, as if afraid to be left alone with me. That evening I sat alone in the family parlor, reading a new collection of poetry by Mr. Rudyard Kipling. Undoubtedly Mrs. Barclay was showing her displeasure by not joining me. Robert was away visiting friends at a neighboring plantation and Rowena obviously didn't dare invite her aunt's wrath by sitting in the same room with me. Rather than minding, however, I found I enjoyed my own company, without Rowena's nervous chatter, Mrs. Barclay's verbal darts, and Robert's eyes watching me, like an apple he expected to fall into his lap any minute.

Around ten o'clock, I put the book aside, and, as was my usual custom since Jason had left for Richmond, I took a stroll in the garden before retiring. I walked slowly up and down the garden paths, a full moon breaking through the clouds lighting my way over the uneven bricks. In the bushes and trees around me a chorus of tree frogs and locusts chanted in chorus while a bobwhite served as counterpoint. Once I stopped to look behind me, at the walls of Fernwood Hall rising pale pink, dreamlike in the moonlight, and its beauty brought a catch to my throat.

How I will hate leaving here, I thought forlornly. Yet I was sure that once Jason Barclay returned and his sister-in-law presented her list of grievances against me, he would have no choice but to dismiss me. Especially since I wasn't fulfilling my duties as a teacher, in any case. What would I do then? I had enough money to see me back to Boston but I doubted if teaching jobs, particularly in the midst of a depression, would be easy to find. Well, there was always Aunt Agnes, as much as I hated the thought of swallowing my pride and turning to her for financial assistance.

I came to a break in the path and realized I had walked farther than I had intended. I was standing at the entrance to Celia's garden. Si and I had pruned back the mock orange and yew so that the summerhouse was no longer hidden from sight. Moonlight made a dappled effect on the white pillars and lacy roof.

As always when I looked at the gazebo, my thoughts returned to Celia Rougier. The picture of her in my mind, however, as an innocent tragic victim was slowly changing. I remembered how Rowena had described her, then Rob and now, Giles. Yet if the truth was that Celia was what they all said, a cold-hearted harlot, a fortune hunter, then why had Jason gone on loving her, even after her death. That brooding pain in Jason's eyes, that at least was real. Suddenly, despite the warmth of the night, I shivered. Suppose I was mistaken. Suppose what I saw in Jason's eyes wasn't pain but the torment of guilt. Suppose what Rowena and Rob and even Giles had insinuated was the truth. It wasn't Brian who had killed Celia, but Jason.

No! I wouldn't believe it. Not Jason. He had loved Celia. But men have killed for love before, I reminded myself. Literature was filled with such tales. If only I knew the truth about Celia . . . was she good or evil . . . fickle or faithful . . . had she deliberately set out to destroy the Barclays or was she an innocent victim of circumstances. If only I knew the truth . . . suddenly remembering something my father had once said, "It's often easier to discover the truth than to live with it." Could I bear to live with the truth that Jason Barclay might be a murderer?

There seemed no answer. At the moment staring at the ethereal summerhouse, shimmering in the moonlight, nothing seemed real, nothing true that I could put my hand to. Not even the night around me. I could swear I had seen a shadow move next to a pillar of the gazebo and yet there wasn't a breath of air stirring.

I jerked erect, peering through the darkness toward the summerhouse. I hadn't been imagining things. The shadow *was* moving. It couldn't be and yet, as I watched, my breath caught in my throat, I saw someone step out from behind a pillar. A shadow separating in half, taking its own form.

The shape of a man in a bright blue cape and jauntily plumed hat. For one moment, evanescent, the figure of the cavalier materialized before my eyes. The great plumed hat shrouded the face but almost I could imagine the sharply drawn features of Brian Barclay beneath the brim. Then the moon slipped behind a cloud, plunging the little garden into darkness. Even in the darkness, though, I knew the figure was still there.

Then I heard the noise, a gliding sound moving over the grass toward me. Until that moment I had been too paralyzed with shock to move. Now fear invaded my body, drove out all logic and reason. All I knew was that I did not dare confront whatever it was slipping toward me, unseen, unimaginable. I whirled and fled.

In my panic I missed the path upon which I had been walking. I darted off onto a side path, leading to an intersection where a sundial suddenly blocked my way. I had to stop to get my bearings. In the daytime I knew every inch of Fernwood's gardens but at night everything looked different.

Did the path to the right lead back to the house or was that the path that led to a cul-de-sac? As I hesitated, trying to make up my mind, I was conscious of the darkness around me, the whispering sound of footsteps, not in a hurry, but slow, deliberate, as if confident of overtaking me.

It had to be the path to the right, I decided, hurrying down it, afraid to look behind, afraid to stop for even a moment. When I struck something hard and cold, I flung out my hands instinctively to keep from falling. Pain throbbed in my knee. Frantically I traced the solid stone beneath my hands, and knew at once where I was. The statue of Pan with his raised flute. This wasn't the path to the house. Pan stood in a yew enclosed circle, a dead end.

I whirled to face the opening through which I had come, my eyes trying to pierce the darkness even as I dreaded what I would see. I could hear that dreadful shuffling sound coming closer, a dank, moldy smell drifting toward me. Whatever it was, was within inches of me, was almost upon me.

With a whimper of despair, I flung myself headlong at the solid wall of yew, trying to claw my way through the needled branches. I thought I screamed for help, then pain ripped my body from head to toe, an explosion of pain, before I sank into oblivion.

I was having a nightmare. I dreamed I was buried alive. Such a vivid nightmare that I could smell the damp earth above me. And in the manner of dreams when I tried to scream for help, I could utter only a faint moan.

It was only a dream, I reminded myself frantically. I need only open my eyes and the nightmare would vanish; I would be safe in my bed. I struggled to sit erect. Why was the room so dark? I didn't remember drawing the curtains. I tried to turn my body and pain, like a vise, gripped my leg and this time I did scream aloud. Pain that was too real to be a dream. And I remembered.

The garden and the shadowy figure in the cape and plumed hat pursuing me. But that had been the garden, I thought, shivering. And this certainly wasn't my bed. There was hard dirt beneath me, a strangely familiar rotten smell in my nostrils.

Carefully I put out my arm, felt solid earth. Horror leaped through me, tearing away my last illusion. I wasn't in the garden or my bedroom. I was buried alive! Not in a coffin and there was some space around me. Fighting off pain and dizziness, I managed to pull myself into a sitting position.

If I could only remember how I had come here, wherever I was. Tentatively I ran my hands over my body. Except for the pain in my right leg and a throbbing at the base of my head, I seemed to be all in one piece. I could see and hear and smell . . . smell. My nose wrinkled at the offensive odor, not damp earth, something else. Rotting apples, moldy cabbage. The cold cellar! Of course, I thought, with a sigh of relief.

But how had I gotten here, I wondered, bewildered. I couldn't remember leaving the cul-de-sac. Had I somehow managed to escape through the yew? At the moment though it didn't matter. What did matter was opening the root cellar doors and climbing out.

I pushed my hands flat against the rough wooden doors over my head. When they didn't move at once, I pushed harder. The doors didn't budge an inch. I kept shoving until splinters of wood drove into the soft flesh of my hands. At last, I sank back exhausted and faced the truth. The cellar doors were bolted on the outside.

And there was no use in shouting for help. The only place I could be heard was the kitchen, and there would be no one there at this time of night. Anyway, did I want to call aloud? Suppose I hadn't escaped from the yew . . . suppose I had been knocked out and brought here, dumped unceremoniously into the cold cellar. If I made too much noise, would whoever it was come back and finish the job?

Uncomfortable as it was, I decided it would be safer to remain quiet. By early morning someone would be at the kitchen, one of the servants, then I would call out. Then I would be safe. I made myself as comfortable as possible, resting my face on my arm against a pile of moldering straw. I managed to doze off occasionally from exhaustion, always jerking awake to a moment of pure terror, with the darkness like walls pressing in upon me, crushing me. Until I remembered. It was all right. I wasn't buried alive. Soon help would come. I was certain to be missed in the morning. I had only to hold on . . . to hold . . . I drifted off again into a light sleep.

Then one time when I jerked awake, I smelled wonderfully fresh, sweet air. A dark shape was standing over me. I cried out in pain and terror. And I heard Rob's voice, "It's all right now, Abigail. Hold on to me."

After that voices blurred. I felt arms lifting me gently, carrying me, the blessed softness of my bed beneath me. Hands moved over my arms and legs, a voice saying, I think Rowena's: "No broken bones, thank goodness."

I sensed rather than saw Charlotte in a voluminous white nightgown, a shadowy figure behind a lamp, her voice shocked, "How do you suppose she fell into the cold cellar?"

"Some idiot left the door open," Rob said.

"No!" I forced my eyes open, forced words to form in my throat, pushed them through my lips. "The cavalier . . . I saw him . . . tried to kill me . . . put me in the cold cellar . . ."

My words echoed against the walls of my tiny bedroom, bounced against the faces gathered around my bed, staring down at me . . . Rowena, Rob, Charlotte . . . all with startled, disbelieving eyes.

CHAPTER TWELVE

"Don't try to talk," Rob said. "You've had a bad fall. Jonas has gone for Dr. Marshall. He'll be here soon."

"No . . ." My voice sounded as if I were far away on the other side of a glass wall from those faces staring at me. "I tell you I saw the cavalier. I ran . . . I couldn't get away."

"What is she saying?" Charlotte pressed closer to the bed. In the lamplight her dark eyes seemed scooped-out hollows in her cheeks.

"She's hysterical. She doesn't know what she's saying."

"Perhaps some brandy," Rowena suggested.

"That's a good idea." Rob left the bedroom and returned with a small glass of brandy. It burned my throat and I pushed it away. But it helped to steady my voice and I tried again to convince the doubting faces.

"You must believe me. He's out there. I saw him. He tried to kill me. Then he put me in the cold cellar and locked the door."

Rob frowned. "The door to the cold cellar wasn't locked, Abigail. It was wide open. I was crossing the garden from the stable to the house and I almost fell into the blasted thing myself."

He's lying, I thought. And yet his face seemed genuinely bewildered. Why? Why should he lie?

"It's fortunate that Cousin Robert came along when he did," Rowena said. "Or you might have lain there in the cold cellar till morning."

"The doors were closed!" My voice rose shrilly. "Closed and locked!"

I struggled to sit up. The pain in my leg made me gasp; a

throbbing at the base of my head like a giant mallet beating inside my skull. Once more there was only darkness.

When I came to again, Rowena and an elderly, white-bearded man stood beside my bed. The man smiled down at me. "I'm Dr. Marshall, Miss Prentice. Are you in much pain?"

"My head and my leg hurts."

He nodded and asked some more questions while he examined me, finally saying, "You must have hit your head when you fell but there doesn't seem to be any concussion. Your leg is badly bruised, probably pulled some muscles. You'll have to favor it for a while."

He poured some medicine from a dark brown bottle into a glass. "The laudanum will help the pain."

I wanted to tell the doctor what had happened. I wanted someone, anyone to believe my story, but the medicine was having an odd effect on me. At first, I felt curiously lightheaded, but then a heavy drowsiness pressed down on me. The words I wanted to say slipped away in my mind like puffs of smoke and I fell asleep.

When I awoke again, the doctor was stretched out asleep in a chair beside the bed and the sun was shining. The doctor awoke when I did, and asked, "Do you remember me, Miss Prentice?"

"Yes, you're Dr. Marshall."

He nodded, pleased. "Good." He lifted my eyelids, peered into my eyes and nodded again. "You're a lucky young lady. How do you feel?"

"Terrible," I said, grimacing as I pushed myself into a seated position. Every muscle in my body ached.

The doctor chuckled. "Well, what do you expect when you roam around the garden at night and tumble into cold cellars."

"I didn't tumble into any cellar," I protested indignantly. "I was hit over the head and put there." I glared at the man. "But then I don't suppose you believe me either."

"Oh, I believe you," the doctor said calmly. "A blow to the head can do strange things to the mind, make you believe all sorts of odd things for a while."

Was it possible, I wondered uneasily. All I could remember

clearly was taking a walk in the garden. Had I somehow stumbled into the open cold cellar, hit my head and the rest, the ghostly figure of the cavalier, my frantic attempt to escape him, was only my mind playing tricks on me. The sunny, familiar look of my bedroom, the bouquet of yellow roses in a vase, the chintz chair by the fireplace, all so normal, so real, made the events of last night seem a vague nightmare from which I had thankfully awakened.

Rowena bustled into the room with a breakfast tray.

"My patient's much better," the doctor told her. "I'd suggest though she stay in bed for a few days. I'll leave the laudanum in case she should have any more pain. Undoubtedly that leg will be bothering her for some time. But only a teaspoonful of laudanum, and not more than once or twice a day," he said warningly.

"All right, doctor, as you say." She placed the tray beside my bed. "I've questioned the servants. They all deny leaving the cellar doors open but, of course, it must have been one of them. I imagine it was Cindy. She gets more forgetful everyday. Will you stay for breakfast, Dr. Marshall?"

"No, thank you, just some of your good coffee and I'll be on my way." He reached for his jacket. "If you should develop any sudden, extreme headaches, Miss Prentice, send for me immediately."

I said I would and thanked him. After Rowena and he left the room, I threw back the coverlet and, cautiously bracing myself against the wrenching pain, managed to crawl out of bed. In my dressing table mirror, I studied my face, dark shadows ringing my eyes and my mouth with a strained hardness that had not been there yesterday. I looked more closely at my reflection, at the tiny cuts on the skin of my face, along my hands and arms, the sort of scratches that yew needles would make, I thought suddenly. Where would I have received cuts like that in a cold cellar? I inched my way over to the chair where the dress I had worn last night had been thrown after Rowena had undressed me.

Picking up the poplin gown, I gave it a shake. From the

pleated skirt and balloon sleeves several yew needles fell to the floor. Then a wave of giddiness swept over me and I barely made it back to my bed. So I hadn't imagined it. Something or someone had frightened me in the garden last night and when I had tried to escape had struck me from behind. The injured leg must have come later when I had been carried to the kitchen garden and dropped into the cold cellar.

My hands twisted at the coverlet, the bitter taste of gall rising in my throat. No, not a ghost, I thought. Although undoubtedly that was what I was supposed to believe. In the first place, I didn't believe in the spirit world, at least, I didn't think I did. Anyway, who ever heard of a ghost who would lock and unlock doors to make the deliberate attempt on my life seem an accidental fall.

But why? Why was I a threat to anyone at Fernwood? Who hated me enough to make such a desperate attempt on my life? And it had to be someone living at Fernwood, someone who knew the story of the ghostly cavalier and was aware of my habit of taking a walk in the garden at night.

Although I wasn't hungry, I forced myself to chew and swallow the hot biscuits dipped in honey, the coddled egg, took swallows of the hot black coffee, hoping it would clear my head. If only I could have glimpsed the face more clearly beneath the plumed hat. At least then I would know who my enemy was. It was the facelessness of the man that made it all so much more . . . evil.

Man. I frowned absently. Why should it necessarily be a man? A woman in the elaborate cavalier's costume, cape, high boots, plumed hat would be easily disguised. And although a woman couldn't have carried me to the cold cellar, I could have been dragged there. Rowena certainly was strong enough, even Mrs. Barclay.

I pushed aside the tray of food, my stomach churning. It was distasteful thinking of the Barclay family this way. That one of them hated me enough to want me dead. Especially when for the next three days they went out of their way to be exceptionally kind to me. Rowena had special dishes cooked to tempt my appetite, Mrs. Barclay brought me an ointment which she said was guaranteed to heal a wrenched joint, and Robert Barclay spent every waking hour he could with me, attentive to my every want, entertaining me with gay stories of his escapades in Richmond that would make me laugh until tears came to my eyes.

We had quickly passed to a first name relationship, and only once did he allude to that night in the drawing room. "Have you forgiven me yet, Abigail?" he asked quietly one afternoon as we sat together on the upstairs veranda. "Not for anything in the world would I willingly cause you a moment's embarrassment or unhappiness."

"There's nothing to forgive," I said, then mischievously, "after all, an experienced swordsman must keep testing his mettle."

He scowled, his voice gloomy. "My exploits with the fair sex are greatly exaggerated." He shrugged indifferently. "Oh, I'll admit I've had my share of conquests, but they've meant nothing to me, a young man sowing his wild oats. But for once, I believe Jason is right. It's time I think of settling down."

At my uneasy stirring, he grinned and pressed my hand gently. "All right, we won't talk about it any more, not while you're still unwell. However, I should warn you, Abigail, my sweet. I'm not a patient wooer."

The third day, over Rowena's objections, I insisted upon joining the family at breakfast. Jonas had fashioned a crude crutch for me, and after breakfast, I decided to attempt a walk in the garden. Somehow I felt that if I could see where I had been attacked, perhaps I could learn something.

I hadn't hobbled more than a few steps when Si appeared beside me. "Miss Rowena sent me to keep an eye on you," he said importantly. "She's afraid you'll get to feelin' poorly."

"Thank you, Si. I just thought I'd look at Miss Celia's garden."

The boy dug his foot into the dust, unhappily, not looking at me. "I ain't been working there, Miss Abigail. Marse Giles says there's more than 'nuf chores to keep me busy at the stable." He added in a rush, "I'd rather help you but Marse Giles, he can be mighty mean when he's crossed."

"It's all right, Si," I assured him. "I understand."

We reached the garden and I rested on the steps of the gazebo, gazing absently at the dark shadows the dogwood flung across the grass. Of course, Giles! Why hadn't I thought of him sooner? I could easily picture him dressing like the cavalier and lying in wait for me in the garden. It was the sort of devilment he would thoroughly enjoy. And he would have no difficulty carrying me to the cold cellar. Yet . . . I bit my lower lip uncertainly. It was a terrible gamble for the plantation manager to take. Giles was no fool. If his ghostly impersonation was discovered, he must know that nothing would save his job at Fernwood. Why should he take such a risk, merely to frighten me? He would need some more urgent, demanding reason.

Then I realized Si was talking, his voice wistful. "Maybe when you're feeling good again, Miss Abigail, you'll help me with my reading."

"I'll give you a lesson right now, Si," I said. "That is, if we had your book."

"I got one right here." Si whipped out a small copy of *McGuffey's Reader* from the waistband of his trousers. As he read aloud, I leaned back against a pillar, correcting him occasionally when he stumbled over a word. It was a relief to pick up the role of teacher and forget the frightening, fruitless questions turning over and over in my mind.

A noise by the mock orange shrubs made me look up. Quentin stood, watching Si and me. His voice was furious. "How come Si can read and I can't?"

Behind his fury, I could sense his frustration, the humiliation of the knowledge that a black servant could read and he couldn't. I felt a twinge of excitement. Perhaps this was the prod Quentin needed to make him want to learn, too.

"Oh, I'm sure you could learn, too, Quentin, if you wanted," I said casually. "Would you like to take lessons again?"

The boy hesitated then nodded, almost belligerently. He stepped forward and arrogantly held out his hand for the book that Si clutched. Si gave me an imploring look and I said quickly, "I'll teach you both together, Quentin. That way you can help each other." Before Quentin could protest, I added, "I'll meet you both in the sitting room tomorrow morning. Now I think I've had enough of an outing for one day." I smiled at Quentin. "Would you help me back to the house?"

Graciously he held out his hand. "You can lean on me, Miss Prentice. I'm lots stronger than I look."

As we walked slowly toward the house, Quentin suddenly blurted, "Is it true, Miss Prentice, that you saw the cavalier . . . you saw the hant?"

I had no doubt the story was already all over the plantation, undoubtedly embellished with each telling. "Not a haunt, Quentin," I said firmly. "Ghosts don't go around hitting people."

"Yes, ma'am, they do." Quentin's voice was low. When I gazed down at him, I was startled at the fixed intensity of his gaze, the frightened despair behind the pale blue eyes. "I saw the cavalier hit my Uncle Guy in the head with a rock."

I stopped short; my knees felt all at once weak. "What are you saying, Quentin? Your Uncle Guy died in a fall from a horse."

The boy shook his head. The words streamed from his mouth as if they had been bottled up too long and it was a relief to let them free at last. "I ran after Uncle Guy that morning. He promised to take me with him into town and he forgot. I took a short cut through the woods so I could meet him at the bridge over the old ice pond. When I reached the edge of the woods, I saw his horse standing without a rider, the reins hanging down. Uncle Guy was lying in the road. The cavalier was there, too, in his blue cape. He had something in his hands, held over his head. When Uncle Guy tried to get up, the cavalier hit him. I could hear the sound the rock made, and Uncle Guy, he just . . . just fell back down. Then the hant, he disappeared. When I ran up, Uncle Guy's head was all bloody . . ."

My fingers bit into the boy's shoulder so that I could feel the shape of the thin bones beneath the flesh. "Don't say any more, Quentin. Why didn't you tell someone? Why didn't you tell your Aunt Charlotte what you saw?"

"I did." The boy turned his face away, his voice sad, defeated. "She didn't believe me. No one believed me. They said I was

making things up again, and one of the servants told me if I
went around telling lies like that the cavalier would come back
and kill me, too." He gave me a half frightened, half relieved
glance. "Only it's you he's after this time, Miss Abigail, not me."

I suddenly felt the throbbing pain in my head returning, all the
unanswered questions I had been trying to avoid thinking about,
jabbing like little knives into my skull. The sick dizziness returned, the ground swaying beneath my feet. Somehow I managed to keep from falling. The boy was terrified enough. I
mustn't scare him further by fainting. "We won't talk about it
any more right now, Quentin," I said. "I'm sure there must be
some logical explanation for what you saw."

"Then you believe me?" he asked happily. "You don't think I
was just making up a story?"

We once more began to walk toward the house, my body
moving slowly, heavily, like an old woman. For God help me,
I did believe Quentin. Not that he had seen a ghost but someone
impersonating the cavalier. The same person who had cold-
bloodedly tried to kill me in the garden three nights before.

CHAPTER THIRTEEN

We had almost reached the house when Mrs. Barclay stepped out the door and, looking around her, spotted Quentin and me advancing slowly up the garden path. She beckoned impatiently. "Come along, Quentin. Your Uncle Jason's home."

The boy looked up at me and I gave him a gentle shove. "Run along. I'll be all right."

After the boy raced off, I stood a moment, uncertain, feeling oddly shy at the thought of seeing Jason Barclay again. Anyway it was family he would be wanting to see right now, not his nephew's tutor. What I had to tell him could wait. I debated whether to return to my room, but I wasn't sure I should chance trying to climb the veranda staircase. My leg already ached from the short walk I had taken. Perhaps it would be best if I sat and rested a few minutes.

I slipped into the rose garden and sat down on a stone bench. Only the hardiest of the roses in the garden had survived the years of neglect, and only a few of these had late summer blooms, a pink damask, a bright scarlet gallica, an old-fashioned moss rose . . .

Even without a wealth of blooms though, it was pleasant in the rose garden, the bees stitching busily through the silence, the sky like blue silk gauze overhead. Except the peacefulness didn't touch the hard core of unease curled deep inside of me.

I wondered what the family was telling Jason about my "accident." I wished I could have told him the whole story myself before the telling could be colored and slanted to appear the workings of an overly imaginative, hysterical female. For, of course, I would have to tell him, no matter the consequences. Jason was entitled to know the truth.

When he suddenly appeared at the entrance to the rose garden, though, a half hour later, I found telling him more difficult than I had anticipated. For one thing I could see at once by the wary look in his eyes that he had been forewarned, and for another, I hadn't expected my heart to lurch and race like a schoolgirl's at sight of him.

He came to stand before me, his voice concerned, "Shouldn't you be resting in your room, Miss Prentice?"

I had forgotten how translucent blue his eyes were so that I felt if I only stared hard and long enough I could see behind them. I forced my voice to a calm composure. "Thank you but I'm practically recovered." I hesitated a moment then asked, "You've been told then about my . . . my injuries?"

Jason's eyes shifted, looked away. "What is there to tell?" he asked uncomfortably. "You went walking in the garden at night. Some imbecile left the cold cellar doors open and you had an accident."

Despite my good intentions, anger sharpened my voice. "No one mentioned my seeing someone in the garden dressed like the cavalier? And that I didn't fall into the cellar but was struck unconscious and locked in there deliberately?"

Jason frowned. "Rowena told me what Dr. Marshall said, that it's not unusual after a blow like you received that you should imagine all sorts of things, even ghosts."

His voice was gentle, soothing, but I could see the disbelief in his face. My hands tightened into fists hidden in the folds of my skirt. I mustn't raise my voice, I thought. The more I sounded like an overwrought female, the less chance I would have to convince Jason. "I didn't imagine I saw a ghost, Mr. Barclay. Perhaps at first when I saw him by the summerhouse, I was too frightened to think clearly then. Now I know it was someone dressed like a cavalier, someone trying to frighten, perhaps even kill me."

Jason lifted a shocked eyebrow. "Surely, Miss Prentice, you realize how incredible that sounds. Why should anyone at Fernwood want to harm you?"

Frustration made my voice tremble. "I don't know why. I

wish I did. At least then it would make some sort of sense." I shook my head helplessly. "There's so much that's happened here at Fernwood that I don't understand, that I haven't been told. For example, why wasn't I told that Quentin saw the cavalier the morning his uncle died?"

Jason's face stiffened warily. "There was no reason to tell you."

"No reason to tell me the truth about Quentin's nightmares? The boy told me he saw the cavalier kill his uncle!"

"That's idiotic!" A burnished red flush spread beneath Jason's tan. "My brother was thrown from his horse and hit his head on a rock in the road. He was killed instantly. Oh, I know what Quentin thinks he saw, but you can't seriously believe him. It was an early March morning, thick with mist. It's true the boy did run after Guy. I suppose the way the mist twisted on the road, some quirk of a child's overactive imagination made him believe he saw a caped figure standing in the road. But Quentin's cavalier was no more real than"—he shrugged—"than the one you think you saw in the garden. Guy's death was an accident."

"Like Celia's death was an accident," I flung the words at him bitterly. "And if I had broken my neck when I was dropped into the cold cellar that would have been an accident, too, wouldn't it?"

The blinding pain that transfigured Jason's face made me flinch inwardly; my hand ached to reach up and smooth that look of anguish from his face. God knows I didn't want to hurt him, not this way.

"No, Celia's death wasn't an accident," he said. "I killed her."

At my shocked look, he sighed and shook his head. "Oh, I didn't literally pull the trigger but I might as well have. We quarreled that night before I went to the party at Silver Grove. I said . . . well, it doesn't matter now, but I must have hurt her deeply. I think she reached the end of her rope that night. She was alone in a strange country with no one to turn to. Perhaps if I had tried harder to understand her . . ."

He shrugged grimly. "But then I knew very little about women.

It was Brian who had the gift. He had only to smile and they fell into his arms, while I stood around, tongue-tied, tangle-footed. I remember how bitter I was when Guy shipped me away to school, away from Fernwood, but then I thought, perhaps if I studied hard, read and learned, if I toured the grand capitals of Europe, perhaps some of the polish, the charm would rub off on me. But, of course, it didn't, just a surface veneer. Nothing had changed underneath. Except, I think I finally accepted the fact that I could never be Brian."

"Did you hate him?" I blurted, and bit my lip, appalled at my asking such a question.

"Hate Brian?" He looked startled. "That would be like hating a part of myself. Oh, I admit there were times I could cheerfully have killed him. Once I almost did. Thank God, Giles was there to pull me away in time. But it was impossible to stay angry with Brian. He charmed everyone, men and women. Why should I have expected it to be different with Celia. It was my fault, not hers. I let pride blind me . . ."

Jason's voice was grief-stricken, his eyes shadowed with a remembered guilt that was like a dagger thrust into my heart. It was clear that Jason had convinced himself that Celia's death was a suicide. Well, how did I know but what he was right? Perhaps the emotional tug-of-war had proven too much for the girl and she had chosen what she might have thought was the easiest way out.

I think I knew then that I could never convince Jason that Celia had been murdered, any more than I could make him believe that I had been deliberately assaulted, his brother, killed. Suddenly I felt exhausted, drained of all emotion except weariness. It was useless. Why should Jason believe me, an outsider? Maybe it was better this way. What right did I have stirring up old pains, old wounds. What was it Giles had said? Let the dead stay buried and forgotten.

I stared down at my hands, knowing that I could not bear to look at Jason and say what I had to say. "Since you've been away, Mr. Barclay, I've come to a decision. I've decided to return to Richmond."

I felt rather than saw his start of surprise. "If it's because of Mrs. Barclay not allowing Quentin to take lessons from you . . ." His voice tightened. "I've had a talk with my sister-in-law. She's agreed that Quentin has recovered his health sufficiently to resume his lessons. As a matter of fact, I confess I was pleased when Quentin himself insisted upon it."

When I still sat quietly, not looking at him, he continued, amused: "As for your second pupil, I told Charlotte it was a tempest in a teapot. Why shouldn't Si be taught if he has the intelligence? I've always thought keeping the blacks in ignorance has caused the South more harm than good."

I still did not speak, afraid to look up, afraid that I might weaken if I did. He waited a moment then said, his voice suddenly harsh, "Of course, if you find your pupil too difficult or if you dislike living here at Fernwood . . ."

Then I did look up. "Oh, no! I've grown very fond of Quentin and I love Fernwood. I'd hate leaving here, leaving . . ."

I stopped myself in time, knowing the truth although I had never dared admit it to myself. It wasn't Quentin or Fernwood. It was Jason Barclay I couldn't bear leaving. Tears stung my eyes. Unwilling to meet Jason's penetrating gaze, afraid that he would see the truth there in my face, I sprang to my feet.

But I had forgotten my bad leg until I put my weight full upon it. Then I gave a gasp of pain, felt myself crumpling, would have fallen if Jason's arms hadn't caught me, pulled me tight against him. At first, I thought I must be imagining it, that the arms around me weren't just supporting but tenderly embracing me, until I heard Jason's voice murmur against my hair, "Don't leave me, Abigail. When I heard about your accident . . . how close I came to losing you, too, I knew then. I can't let you go."

His lips traced a path from my temple, caressed my cheek then reached for my mouth. When Rob had kissed me, I had felt a sense of shock. It wasn't that way with Jason. Rather as if I had somehow always known how it would feel to fit into the curve of his arms, my mouth knowing instinctively the shape, the touch of his against mine.

When he finally stepped away, his arms loosening but still not releasing me, we both simply stared, startled, at each other, to find the same longings reflected in each other's eyes. Jason's voice was filled with wonder. "Do you know in Richmond I kept looking for you. I would read an article in the paper and think, I must discuss this with Abigail. Or I'd see something in a shop window and turn to show it to you, hoping to see you smile. Did you know I used to sit, waiting for your smile, those evenings in the parlor? You have such a serious, intent look and when you smile, your face would suddenly be open with delight as a child's. I never thought I could miss anyone so much. Or that you could feel the same."

Once more his lips sought mine and this time it was I who finally pulled away, breathless, scrambling for safe ground. Everything was happening too quickly.

"You will marry me, Abigail. We can tell the family tonight."

"No." At Jason's eyes narrowing, uncertain, I said quickly, "We have to give them time to become accustomed to the idea. After all, they hardly know me, Mr. Barclay."

"Jason," he corrected me, smiling, and then his smile fading, he said slowly, "It's not Celia. You're not thinking about Celia."

I put my hand to his mouth, silencing him. "We won't talk about Celia again," I said firmly. "It's just . . . I need a little time."

"Of course." He looked disappointed but nodded. "We'll wait then but not too long, Abigail. Don't make me wait too long. Now I'll take you back to the house. You shouldn't be standing on that leg."

That evening at supper though, no matter how Jason and I tried to hide what had happened in the rose garden that morning, it must have been only too evident to the assembled Barclay family when they looked into Jason's face and my own.

After the meal, I excused myself and went to my room, thinking that it would be better if Jason spoke to his family without my presence. To my surprise, I found Rob waiting for me in the upstairs hall, his face dark with anger. "So Jason's won again," he said bitterly. "First, Brian lost to him and now, me."

"Don't be silly, Rob," I said sharply. "There was nothing between us for you to lose."

"Are you so sure of that, Abby?" he asked, smiling, his voice husky. "When I kissed you, you felt nothing, nothing at all?"

My face grew warm, remembering.

"And Celia," he continued, pinpoints of devilment dancing in his eyes. "Celia doesn't worry you at all, how she died."

"Jason told me about that. Celia committed suicide."

Rob threw back his head and laughed. "Celia commit suicide? Oh, come now, Abigail, didn't you know? Celia was shot through the head. What beautiful woman would ever kill herself by shooting herself point blank in the face?"

CHAPTER FOURTEEN

I felt suddenly, almost physically ill at the picture Rob's words conjured in my mind. Then I saw Charlotte Barclay coming down the hallway, her eyes fastening curiously on Rob and me standing together in what must seem a clandestine conversation. Turning hastily, I pushed open the door to the blue bedroom. "Good night, Rob," I said, without looking at him.

After undressing quickly, I climbed into my chintz-covered bed, hesitated a moment, then determinedly extinguished the lamp beside the bed. Ever since the evening of my fall into the cold cellar, I had kept a small light burning beside my bed. I forced myself not to think of that night, to remember instead the warmth of Jason's arms, their strength encircling me as if nothing evil could ever touch me . . . finally I fell asleep. And awoke in the middle of the night, my heart pounding. In my nightmare I dreamed that I had been once again relentlessly pursued by the faceless cavalier, smelled the dank odor of earth in my nostrils, felt again the terror of being buried alive. And the darkness, the unending blackness . . .

Trembling, I reached for the lamp beside my bed, almost knocked it over, caught it, and lit the wick, breathing a great sigh of relief as the comforting yellow light spread throughout the room. I started to lean back against my pillows when I stopped, frowning at the door to the blue bedroom. I could have sworn the door had been shut when I went to bed. Now it stood slightly open.

I stared at the black slit in the doorway. Well, obviously I hadn't closed the door as tightly as I had thought and just as obviously I wouldn't be able to fall back asleep until it was closed again. I went over to the door and reached out my hand for the gold embossed doorknob, bracing myself for the inevitable disagreeable, mildewed smell that always hung over the room. My nose twitched, startled. It couldn't be and yet I would swear I caught the faint fragrance of roses. A spicy sweet scent so real that I turned back to my room to see if somehow miraculously a bouquet of roses had appeared.

But there was no bouquet of roses in my bedroom, and, as I took the lamp from my bedside and lifted it before me so that it shone into the adjoining bedroom, no bouquet of roses in the blue bedroom either. Only the heavy, ornate furniture, the towering black carved bed, the massive wardrobe, the gold candlesticks on the mantel with cherubs at their bases, a fragile ormolu clock on the dressing table. No roses. No flowers at all.

All at once, I felt gooseflesh rising on my arms, as if I were standing in a draft. The clammy chill always present in the bedroom seemed to be centering right around me. My limbs felt heavy in the vortex of that chill, my body for a moment helpless, unable to move, the way I had felt for a few seconds in the garden when I had seen the cavalier step away from the gazebo. The shadow my lamp cast moving across the bedroom floor was like a wavering shape without form or substance, reminding me of the cavalier, too. No, I thought suddenly, not the cavalier, a slimmer, more graceful figure. And all at once the fragrance of roses in my nostrils was too cloyingly sweet, the chill surrounding me like moist hands stroking my skin.

Abruptly I retreated to my bedroom, closing the door behind me firmly. And as I climbed, shivering, back into the cozy warmth of my bed. I scolded myself roundly. That's what came of listening to Rowena and her servants' tales, I thought. If she hadn't mentioned about Jason's always keeping Celia's bedroom filled with roses, I would never have imagined I smelled them there tonight. And I certainly wasn't foolish enough to believe that some fragment or residue of Celia's spirit, unable to rest, still lingered in that blue bedroom. After all, I had been through the blue bedroom many times before and never noticed the fragrance. If Celia wanted to haunt the room where she had died, why wait till tonight?

Because I hadn't been engaged to Jason before tonight, I thought suddenly. Because I hadn't threatened to take Jason away from her before tonight.

I groaned and buried my face in the pillow. Now I was being as superstitious as the servants. Celia was dead. And the scent of roses was only that, not a jealous spirit returning from the other world.

Nevertheless, I once again let the lamp beside my bed burn all night.

The next morning I made a point of walking slowly through the blue bedroom to the hallway. The room was dark shadowed with a musty odor, as usual, and if there were a scent of roses, it was so faint as to be almost indistinguishable. A window was opened several inches though, I noticed, and below the window in the kitchen garden there was a small rosebed with a few roses blooming. It didn't seem possible the fragrance could reach to the second floor window but still a sudden breeze might have wafted the scent upward.

Feeling oddly relieved, I went on down to breakfast. Rowena announced that Jason had already left for the fields. "He's decided to start cutting the tobacco as soon as possible. The price of tobacco is dropping in Richmond every day, he said."

Guiltily I remembered I hadn't even thought to ask Jason how his business in Richmond had gone, but Rowena didn't seem interested in volunteering any more information and I decided to wait and ask Jason myself.

Charlotte and Quentin hadn't returned from their morning ride by the time I finished breakfast and while I waited, I strolled into the drawing room, drawn as if by a magnet to the portrait of Brian Barclay. That amused gaze seemed to be watching me as closely as I was studying him. If only, I thought exasperated, he looked more like a murderer. I sighed to myself. But then I suppose murderers seldom do look the part.

"There you are, Miss Prentice." Mrs. Barclay, still wearing her black riding gown and carrying a silver-handled whip, walked into the room. "Quentin is waiting for you in the sitting room." Then, as if in reluctant acknowledgment of my changed status: "Or perhaps you'll no longer be teaching Quentin, now that you and Jason have . . . have come to an understanding."

She can't even force herself to say the words, I thought wryly . . . now that Jason and I are to be married. I was too happy this morning though to bear grudges, and undoubtedly it must have been a shock for Charlotte Barclay to hear the news.

I made my voice conciliatory. "I realize it must seem very sudden, my engagement to Mr. Barclay."

"I kept company with Guy Barclay for two years before we announced our engagement," she said, her voice cool. "I'm old-fashioned enough to believe that hasty engagements are usually unfortunate for all concerned."

Was she thinking of Celia, I wondered. Jason couldn't have known the French girl very long before they became engaged. Then, impulsively, I asked, "Are there any pictures of Mademoiselle Rougier here at Fernwood?"

"No, not that I know of. Why do you ask?"

"Rob said . . . well, that I resembled her."

Charlotte glanced at me thoughtfully. "Perhaps a little, in the coloring, but Celia Rougier was a strikingly beautiful woman. I've never seen eyes so dark and lustrous. She used belladonna, I imagine, to make them shine that way. And her skin was almost too white. There are things, you know, a woman can do. There was a great belle in Richmond before the war. She took small doses of arsenic to keep her complexion pale."

"Celia couldn't help being beautiful," I protested, wondering why I continually seemed to rise to the young woman's defense.

"Oh, I tried to like her, for the family's sake, I tried." Mrs. Barclay's voice was soft, petulant. "It was plain to me though from the beginning what she was doing, deliberately turning brother against brother. And it wasn't as if she cared for any of them. But they were too blind, too dazzled by her, to see what she was doing. But I saw. I knew. Underneath that charm, she hated us. She hated every one of us."

Mrs. Barclay's lovely face contorted in memory, her delicate hands tearing at the fragile lace handkerchief she held. "I've never told anyone before but that last night, I went to her room. I begged her to leave Fernwood before it was too late. She laughed at me. She said I was jealous because I couldn't give Guy children and she planned to have babies, lots of sons to carry on the Barclay name. I can see her still, smiling, taunting me, saying 'Jason and I will make beautiful babies.' Oh, she was vulgar, wicked. But she gave wickedness and evil such a brightness and sparkle that it seemed exceedingly attractive. She deserved to die!"

Speaking softly, as if afraid I might break the spell, I asked, "Then you don't think her death was an accident? You think Brian . . ."

But the spell was broken. Her eyes stared through me contemptuously. "Brian? Of course not. He was too much of a gentleman to lift his hand in violence against a woman, no matter how base and coarse the creature." She hesitated then said quickly, "Her death was an accident, a providential accident. It does happen, you know. Evil is destroyed and righteousness triumphs."

She turned her gaze toward the portrait of her brother-in-law. "Poor Brian. Who would have thought it would end this way. He was always the golden son, the one who had so much to offer, so much to live for. Instead, it's Jason who's won. Celia's death rid him of a woman who would have made him a particularly unhappy marriage. Guy's death brought him control of Fernwood. And now . . ." She broke off abruptly, her voice lightly malicious. "Still it's rather like it was then, isn't it? Two brothers in love with the same woman."

Before I could protest, she turned imperiously and swept from the room, reminding me, "Don't forget, Quentin's waiting."

I sighed and turned my gaze back to Brian. At least, I could agree partly with Mrs. Barclay. It was difficult to believe that this man would raise his hand against a woman. The gentleness in the face, the teasing good humor in the mouth. How alive he seemed! And not at all frightening. Certainly not like the face-less cavalier that had pursued me in the garden, the sense of evil that seemed to emanate from that stalking figure. And yet the costume was the same, the blue velvet cape, the plumed hat.

I leaned forward, taking a closer look at the costume. It was the same, exactly the same! Where had the cavalier in the garden secured his costume? Very likely, it was the same clothes that Brian had posed in years before. If so, where was the costume now? The plumed hat, bulky cape, couldn't be easy to hide.

As I went to teach Quentin and Si, the excitement of the idea grew within me. Suppose I should find the costume hidden in one of the bedrooms here at Fernwood. Wouldn't that at least prove to Jason that I hadn't imagined seeing the cavalier? That the costume in fact did exist. If nothing else, it would warn me who my enemy was here at Fernwood so that I could be on my guard.

As soon as I finished the morning lesson, I decided to begin the search. The undertaking, however, wasn't that simple. I had to wait two days before I could gain access to the bedrooms without being seen, first Rowena's. Her dresses were hung neatly in the wardrobe, the rest of her clothes folded in a lavender scented chifforobe. At the bottom of a drawer, hidden beneath a cashmere shawl, was a slim book of poetry. In front of the book was an inscription, laboriously written: *Your devoted friend, Samuel Watkins.* Several dried violets were pressed between the pages.

I felt a wave of distaste at my prying into someone else's private life. Hastily I replaced the book and clothes and left the room.

My feelings of aversion, however, did not stop me from examining the other bedrooms at Fernwood, and finding noth-ing. No cavalier's costume, nothing even slightly resembling it. The other rooms of Fernwood, the drawing room, dining room, library, sitting rooms, contained no trunk or closets large enough to contain the costume. As a last resort I checked Quentin's room though with his fear of the cavalier, it seemed the last place the costume would be found.

There remained finally the kitchen and other outbuildings and, of course, Giles's room. I purposely left his room for last because the idea of returning there, even with the owner absent, made my flesh crawl. I decided to investigate the kitchen first. I had hoped the building would be deserted but I was wrong. A lanky brown-haired man stood by the fireplace talking to Rowena. Rowena's back was toward me and they were speaking too quietly for me to hear what they were saying. When the man saw me, he stopped talking at once, and Rowena whirled around, her face turning a sickly pale. I said, embarrassed, "I'm sorry, I didn't mean to intrude. I didn't know you had company."

Reluctantly Rowena introduced the man. "Miss Prentice . . . Mr. Watkins. Mr. Watkins was just . . . just leaving."

I remembered the inscription in the poetry book, the Sam Watkins that had been discussed the first night at the dinner table. What had Rob called him . . . poor white trash. To me, the man had a coarse, kindly face, as sun burned red as the soil he tilled, and although apparently ill at ease, he stood with a braced sort of simple dignity.

"I'll be on my way." He almost stumbled over a chair in his haste to leave the room.

I felt as if I owed Rowena an apology. "I'm sorry your friend couldn't stay. I hope I didn't . . ."

Rowena looked as if she were about to burst into tears, her voice choked, "Sam Watkins is not my friend. He was delivering chickens for our dinner." She spoke with a suppressed bitterness that was more alarming than anger. "Before the war, the Watkins children went barefoot summer and winter and never saw the inside of a school. Somehow Sam Watkins scraped together enough money after the war to buy a piece of Barclay land. But that doesn't give him the right to come to the front door of Fernwood."

I stared at Rowena, exasperated. I had seen the Watkins

farm on one of my morning rides. It was a neat, well kept farmhouse. "If you care for the man," I demanded, "why don't you marry him? Why let foolish pride stand in your way?"

A mottled redness stained Rowena's throat. "Pride! What do you know of pride?" she almost hissed. "At least, I've too much pride to accept a man who proposes to me the minute he learns I've become an heiress."

Bewildered, I stared at Rowena. What was she talking about?

She reached into her apron pocket, brought out a letter and thrust it into my hand. It was addressed to me at Mrs. Carson's boardinghouse in Richmond and was postmarked Boston, Massachusetts, some weeks before. The letter was written with a legal conciseness. The firm of Renshaw and Brooks, Attorneys-at-Law for the estate of Agnes Bailey, herewith informed me of the death of my aunt after a lingering illness, and that according to the terms of her will, and as her only living relative, I was the sole heir of her estate, moneys, and properties. Although the final figure of the worth of the estate was not yet known, the value was estimated to be close to one-half million dollars.

With one part of my mind, I felt a sense of relief. So that was why Aunt Agnes had never written me after father died, not through spite but because she had been too ill. At the same time, I felt guilty that even with the enormity of the inheritance, I could still feel no great affection for the woman.

Then, puzzled, I looked up at Rowena. "I don't understand. How did you get this letter?"

"I was cleaning Jason's room the morning after he returned from Richmond. I emptied his satchel to see if any of his clothes needed washing. I found the letter at the bottom of the bag." She stared at me defiantly. "It was already opened."

I licked my mouth. My lips felt parchment dry, as if they would crack if I moved them.

Rowena's eyes darted nervously away from my face. "I'm sorry," she said sullenly. "I shouldn't have told you. Anyway, it isn't that Jason isn't fond of you. I'm sure he is."

I didn't wait to hear any more. I turned and hurried as fast as my leg would allow toward the fields where I knew Jason was working. At the bridge over the ice pond, I rested a minute. The water beneath the bridge was almost completely covered now by a green, slimy scum. A fetid smell drifted up to me from the pond. I turned my head away and hurried on again.

I could see the workers in the fields now. They had already begun the cutting, stepping carefully around the large sand leaves that were yellowing in the sun on the ground. Jason saw me and walked quickly toward me, hands outstretched, a broad smile on his face.

"Abigail, you shouldn't have walked this far . . ."

"I have to speak to you."

He glanced at my face then said, "All right." He nodded toward a curing shed. "We'll be alone there."

I followed him into the dark vastness of the shed. The sickly sweet scent of tobacco filled the air, as if the very wood were permeated with the odor.

Almost as soon as we stepped inside, I asked, "When you went to Richmond, Jason, was it because of financial problems?"

If he was startled at my question, he gave no sign. He spoke slowly, "I hadn't wanted to tell you but I suppose you should know the truth. I arrived in Richmond too late. The bank where the Barclays have always kept their funds had gone under the day before. The rail stocks that Charlotte brought to Guy when she married him are practically worthless because of the panic."

Jason waved his hand around him, his voice weary. "The house . . . land and the tobacco . . . that's all the Barclays have left. As it is these last few years, I've been operating on a shoestring." He shrugged ruefully. "You won't be marrying into a wealthy family, my dear."

"But you will, won't you, Jason?" I said bitterly and handed him the letter from the attorneys.

He read it quickly, then glanced up. For a moment I thought I glimpsed something deep in his eyes, anger, shock . . . I could not tell which, but then they were once more cold, remote. I had the feeling that although we stood very close he had physically moved away from me. "When did you receive this letter?" he asked carefully.

"I didn't receive it. It was found, opened, hidden in your satchel." My voice trembled, broke in spite of myself. "Did you run into Mrs. Carson in Richmond, Jason? Did she ask you to deliver the letter to me, and you couldn't resist opening it. Is that why your very first day home, you asked me to marry you, because of that letter?"

Jason handed the letter back to me. His voice was flat, almost disinterested. "Since you already seem to know the answers to your questions, there doesn't seem any point in discussing this further."

I stared into his face, the muscles pulled taut giving his features a curiously blank expression and only the blue eyes were alive, charged with an icy fury. I wondered if he had looked that way the night he had seen Celia and Brian together in the summerhouse.

Then I turned and walked out of the curing shed into the hot, glaring sunlight, lifting my face into its crushing heat as if it could burn away the pain and humiliation. I limped back down the road, Jason's words jiggling in my mind, like dust motes. When I reached the house, the back of my dress was stuck damply to my body. I went up to my room to change and discovered in my absence, my clothes and belongings had been transferred from the tiny bedroom to the large blue bedroom, obviously, according to Mrs. Charlotte's sense of propriety, a more fitting room for a Barclay bride-to-be.

At least, the furniture had been polished, the windows opened wide to freshen the air and a bowl of yellow roses placed beside the huge black walnut bed. I felt an insane desire to laugh but knew I didn't dare, or the misery welling up inside me would dissolve into a flood of tears.

Forcing back the tears, I bathed myself with the pitcher of cool water left on the washstand. In the mirror above the stand my face looked drawn, the skin sallow, my eyes dull. What a fool I was, I thought in sudden bitterness, to actually deceive myself into believing that I was pretty, that I was even able to compete with the beauteous Celia Rougier. Why hadn't it once occurred to me to wonder at Jason's returning from Richmond and suddenly, miraculously being overwhelmed by my charms. After years of arid spinsterhood how could I have believed that overnight I had become the sort of enchantress with whom men impetuously fall in love. But, of course, the answer was simple. I had believed it because I wanted to believe it.

I didn't go down to supper that night. Dulcy brought a tray to my room. She didn't look at me directly as she served me. I suspected that not only Rowena but Charlotte Barclay and Rob—and undoubtedly now even the servants—knew about the letter. That Jason had asked me to marry him only because of the inheritance.

I was too unhappy to eat and pushing aside the tray, went through the little sitting room and down into the garden for a breath of air. In the moonlight the red roses looked black, the moonflower blossoms by the terrace an unearthly white. I didn't stroll far from the terrace. I had no desire to chance the pathways of the garden again alone at night.

"Enjoying the evening air, Miss Prentice? And a fine night it is."

Giles had come up quietly. As I turned to face him, he smiled tauntingly. "I'm surprised you aren't afraid of bumping into your ghost friend. Or was it Brian Barclay that you saw? They do say a murderer never rests quiet in his grave."

My own unhappiness weighed too heavily on me to leave room for fear of this man. "Perhaps it wasn't Brian that killed Mademoiselle Rougier . . . or Jason either."

And felt a thrill of triumph knowing that my words had struck home. Giles's eyes narrowed beneath the shaggy brows till they seemed to disappear. An undercurrent of anger, and yes, fear, thickened his voice. "And who else would be interested in killing that worthless woman?"

"You're forgetting Mrs. Charlotte and Miss Rowena were here," I said. Then, my heart pounding, wondering if I were being too foolhardy, "And there's only your word that you weren't at Fernwood Hall that night."

"Who says I was here?" he demanded belligerently. "If it was Miss Rowena, she lies. Mrs. Charlotte saw Brian riding away after he shot the woman."

"She didn't hear the shot that killed Celia though. What if Celia was still alive when Brian left? Alive and defenseless with only two women in the house to protect her."

I had gone too far. Giles's face pushed close to mine. "It's lies, all lies! You think I'm fool enough to dirty myself with the likes of her?" A blind, savage fury crept into his voice, the rough hands lifted, curled on either side of my neck, not quite touching the skin. "I'd not be needing fancy pistols either," he gloated softly.

Instead of fear, I felt only a raw anger, to think that those hands should dare to touch me. I stood very still within the circle of those green tipped fingers, my voice icy. "If you don't step aside immediately, Mr. Latham, I'll scream so loudly, I promise you everyone in the house will hear me."

For a moment a look of grudging admiration touched the milky blue eyes. Then the hands fell away. He swayed and muttered, "You would, too. You're like her, that way. She had brass gall, she did, to come here and try and get away with her scheme, knowing what would happen to her if anyone found out. I give her that. She had more guts than any of the mealy-mouthed females in this family ever had. Barclay money didn't buy her in the end. Yes, you're like her. Be careful you don't end up the way she did with her pretty face in the dirt."

He backed away, scowling, as if suddenly realizing he was talking too much. Then he wheeled and left me, standing alone in the garden. Now that he was gone all at once I began to tremble.

CHAPTER FIFTEEN

Giles didn't return to the stable. I could hear his footsteps heading toward the road that led into the fields, probably taking the shortcut into the town of Crossroads. I had heard enough servants' gossip to know that the plantation manager often spent his evenings, drinking with his cronies in town. It occurred to me that if this were the case, then tonight would be the ideal time to search Mr. Latham's room. Except . . . I remembered tardily, why should I bother now? Celia Rougier's death, the ghostly cavalier were no longer any of my concern. After what had happened between Jason and me, I wouldn't be staying on at Fernwood. As soon as my leg was well enough for me to travel . . .

But even as I thought this, I was limping toward the stable, because I was remembering something else. I wasn't the only one at Fernwood terrified of the ghostly cavalier. There was Quentin who lived in deadly fear of the apparition he had seen kill his uncle.

My feet faltered when I stepped into the pitch blackness of the stable and I had to fumble along the wall until I located the lantern. After I lit it, I made my way awkwardly up the narrow staircase, the horses, restless in their stalls, nickering softly below me.

Giles's door was unlocked and I stepped quickly inside. There were only two places I could search, the old-fashioned wardrobe and the wooden trunk sitting in a corner of the room. The wardrobe contained only work clothes and one well-tailored suit for special occasions. The trunk had a lock upon it but the lock was not set. When I opened the lid, there was an odor of mothballs. Then I was digging into a pile of stored woolen blankets. Disappointment cut through me. Half-heartedly I continued thrusting my hand down one side of the trunk, the coarsely woven wool scratching at my skin. Then stopped, as if I had been bitten. That wasn't wool I had felt for just a moment. It was something velvety soft. In a few seconds I had tossed the blankets onto the floor. At the very bottom of the trunk I found what I was seeking, a blue velvet cape, a plumed felt hat with the feathers crushed, a pair of black high top boots, mud-smeared, and a rust-caked sword.

I don't remember leaving Giles's room or hurrying as fast as I could limp through the kitchen garden, the costume held awkwardly in my arms. I do remember the shocked looks on the faces of the Barclays as I burst through the French door into the sitting room where they were gathered. The heavy sword clattered to the floor as words poured incoherently from my mouth.

It was Jason who crossed to my side, gave my shoulders a shake. "Get hold of yourself, Abigail," he said sharply. "You're not making sense. What are you doing with those old clothes?"

I took a deep, ragged breath. "The cavalier's costume—I found it in Giles's room. The person I saw dressed in a cavalier's costume in the garden, it must have been Giles. He was the one who tried to kill me."

"Oh, come now, Abby," Rob drawled. "I admit old Giles is something of a reprobate but why should he want to kill you?"

"I don't know why. Unless . . ." My voice halted, for suddenly I did know. Wasn't it too much of a coincidence that it was after my conversation with Giles in his room, when he realized that I wouldn't be content until I solved the mystery surrounding the death of Celia, that the ghost had appeared in the garden and attacked me. "Unless he was afraid I might discover how Celia Rougier really died," I finished slowly.

I heard Rowena give a little gasp but I plunged forward because it was too late now, in any case, to turn back. "I'm sure Giles knows more about that night than he's ever told. He may have even killed Celia himself."

"That's enough, Abigail." Jason's face was flushed. I could tell he was struggling to hold on to his temper. "You're too upset to know what you're saying. I told you how Celia died."

"No." My leg was aching and I longed to sit down but I didn't dare for fear that my courage would drain away, like stuffing from a broken doll. "Don't you see, Jason, as long as you keep pretending Celia's death was a suicide, as long as you won't face the truth, she'll never be dead. She's more of a ghost haunting Fernwood than the cavalier ever could be."

Jason frowned impatiently. "Giles wasn't even here at Fernwood the night Celia died."

"Yes, he was." Rowena's face turned a dull flustered red as all eyes turned to her. "I saw him," she said defiantly. "It was shortly after I had gone to bed. I heard a horse ride up the drive and I saw that it was Giles. His horse was lathered as if he had been riding hard. He went around to the stable and a few minutes later he came back with a fresh horse and rode away."

"For God's sake, Rowena, why didn't you say something sooner?" Rob's voice was disgusted.

The mottled red spread to Rowena's neck. "I didn't see where it made any difference. He didn't come into the house and Celia was alive when he rode away. Her bedroom door was open and I could hear her and Aunt Charlotte argu— talking," she amended quickly.

But I knew why she hadn't said anything. Giles must have warned her not to, and Rowena was afraid of Giles in the same way the black servants were, afraid of how he might get back at her if she crossed him.

Mrs. Barclay had been listening, now she spoke quietly. "I don't see why you shouldn't, at least, question Giles," she said to Jason. "I've told you all along that I never liked that man."

"I agree with Charlotte." Rob gave his brother a derisive, lazy smile. "Unless there's some reason why you don't want to find out the truth about that girl's death."

For a moment I thought Jason was going to protest further,

then he shrugged, his voice cold. "Very well, I'll talk to Giles in the morning. Will that satisfy all of you?"

I flinched inwardly as his gaze fastened at last on me, as if, I thought appalled, he hated me. His eyes were like chips of ice, with no warmth in them at all.

It was late that night before I fell asleep, a light, restless sleep. Once I awoke when I thought I heard the sound of voices outside the window, a man's drunken singing. I suddenly remembered that in my excitement I had left the blankets flung down in Giles's room. He couldn't help but know that someone had searched his room, found the costume. It didn't matter, I told myself. When Jason questioned the plantation manager in the morning, Giles would know his masquerade had been discovered in any case.

I overslept the next morning. When I hurried down to breakfast, I met Rowena in the hall, her face pulled into its perpetually worried look. "If you're looking for Jason, he's already left for the fields."

"Did he talk to Giles?" I asked eagerly.

"I don't think so. I heard Dulcy tell him that Giles didn't show up for breakfast this morning. Of course, he seldom does, after spending a night in town," Rowena said, with a sniff of disapproval. "Jason said he couldn't wait and left without him."

Well, at least, Jason had asked for Giles, I thought hopefully. I had wondered if, in the cold light of dawn, Jason might not have second thoughts about questioning the plantation manager. After morning class, when it must have been obvious to even my two students that my thoughts were elsewhere, I decided not to wait any longer but ride out to the fields and talk to Jason. It had been an overcast morning but the sun was just beginning to break through as I started out. I could still see the gray trails of mist ahead of me, hanging low in the hollows of the road, tangled in the Queen Anne's lace and the creepers along the bottom of the rail fence. Soon the sun would be blazing uncomfortably but right now, one could almost sense the coming of fall, a tartness in the air like biting into a crab apple.

As my mare approached the bridge over the ice pond, I noticed that the wooden surface had a thin glaze of moisture and the horse stepped nervously. Glancing absently down toward the water, I saw that a large willow limb had fallen into the slimy surface. Its pronged, twisted branches snagged leaves and marsh grass in its bony grip.

Suddenly I leaned forward in the saddle, the reins falling from my nerveless hands. Something heavy and dark like a cloth bundle was caught against the willow branch, floating, a shapeless bulk on the pea-green slime.

It was only some old clothes, I told myself, a man's suit thrown away as useless. Nevertheless, I was dismounting, limping toward the water's edge . . . for who in this poverty-stricken countryside threw away clothes, no matter how worn?

I was so near the pond now that the toe of my boot disturbed the motionless surface of the water. A ripple floated out to the willow branch. My heart squeezed painfully. From the bundle of cloth, I saw a hand floating, rising, and falling effortlessly, as if reaching for the branch.

My placid mare looked back at me with astonishment as I mounted again, laid the whip to her flank and sent her racing down the road to the tobacco fields. The workers by the curing shed lifted dark, questioning faces to me as I cried, "Come help me, hurry! There's a man in the ice pond."

Jason and Rob appeared at the entrance to the curing shed; Jason gave orders and he and Rob disappeared down the road with several of the workers. I waited, climbing off of my mare but clinging to the reins, as if for support.

A half hour later Rob came for me with the carriage. He tied my horse to the rear of the carriage then gently lifted me inside.

"It was Giles, wasn't it?" I asked.

Rob nodded. His face was ashen.

"Perhaps if I had pulled him out right away," I reproached myself even as I cringed at the thought of touching that slime-coated hand, with the green stained fingertips clutching at the willow.

Rob shook his head. "It wouldn't have helped. He was already dead."

We passed over the bridge and I looked quickly away but I needn't have bothered. The body was gone. Only a few of the field hands still stood around, talking among themselves, giving the carriage a curious glance as it passed.

In the library Rowena and Mrs. Charlotte sat waiting. When we came in, Rowena asked eagerly, "What happened? All we could get from Jason was that Abigail found Giles's body in the ice pond."

"Giles was a good swimmer," Mrs. Charlotte remarked, almost absently. "I remember he taught Quentin."

"No one knows what happened." Rob poured himself a stiff drink from the whiskey decanter. "I suppose Giles came home drunk last night, slipped, fell off the bridge and drowned."

Rowena's mouth set primly. "Giles always did drink too much. A man his age, it certanly wasn't good for him."

Rob managed a weak smile. "Well, at least the old fox died happy. Drunk as a coot, he probably never knew what happened."

And I'll never find out now what Giles knew about Celia's death, I thought suddenly. Or if it was Giles who had paraded around Fernwood masquerading as the cavalier. Then felt ashamed of myself. The man was dead. Whatever evil he had done had died with him. Somehow Rob's words seemed too glib at a time like this.

Mrs. Barclay must have thought so, too. She got to her feet, giving her brother-in-law a cold glance. "I find your tone of voice most disrespectful, Robert. A man lies dead. And death is never a matter for jest. I'm going to break the news to Quentin. I'm afraid he'll take it very hard."

For the first time since I met Charlotte Barclay, she looked her age, her cheeks sunken, her skin gray-looking above the black high-necked collar of her dress. Her shoulders were drooping, not held proudly erect, as she slowly left the room.

"Where's Jason?" Rowena asked after her aunt left.

"He went to town for the sheriff."

"The sheriff! But why? It was an accident," Rowena said firmly. "Why should the sheriff be called into it?"

"He'll have to see the body," Rob explained patiently. "It's only a formality."

Later that afternoon the sheriff arrived, a heavy-set man with a simple, open face and work-roughened hands, looking vaguely uncomfortable in the walnut-paneled library.

He questioned me first. I explained how I happened to find the body, and that the last time I had seen Giles Latham alive had been early last evening. "We exchanged a few words," I said. "Then he went down the path toward the fields, I presumed into town."

"There's no doubt he was in town last night," the sheriff nodded. "We got plenty of witnesses, including Willy Todd. Giles beat up Willy in a fight at the tavern. Drunk as old Giles was I'm surprised he made it as far as the pond. Dr. Marshall says most of the bruises we found on Giles are from the fight he got into, but there's one bad cut that must have been made when he fell off the bridge into the water. There's a jagged rock below the surface near where we found him. If he struck the rock and wasn't killed instantly, the water there is deep enough to cause his death by drowning before he got his senses back."

He turned to Jason. "You and your brother here"—he jerked a finger toward Rob—"you didn't see anything when you went to the fields this morning?"

"We didn't go over the bridge," Jason explained. "We went around by the toll road to the Watkins place. Sam's offered the use of some of his hands to help with the cutting of our tobacco."

"You didn't see Giles at all last night?"

Jason hesitated a moment then shook his head. "No."

"And you, Mrs. Barclay?" The sheriff's voice softened, filled with respect as he faced the older woman. "One of the stable-boys tells me you and young Quentin often take a ride to the fields in the mornings."

She gave a delicate shudder. "I did ride over the bridge,

Sheriff. Fortunately Quentin wasn't with me. He stayed at the hall this morning. I didn't happen to look down into the pond. I came back by way of the toll road."

"Miss Rowena? You didn't see Giles either?"

Rowena shook her head. "Giles didn't take breakfast this morning." The tip of her nose pinkened. "But that wasn't too unusual. It never occurred to me that he might not have made it home at all."

Suddenly, as if remembering a dream, a snatched memory came to me of being awakened in the night by a voice drunkenly singing. It couldn't have been Giles though. He had never made it as far as his room last night.

Something of my bewilderment must have shown in my face for the sheriff asked quickly, "Was there anything you wanted to add, Miss Prentice?"

I asked hesitantly, "I was wondering, Sheriff, how you could tell how long . . . how long Mr. Latham had been in the water?"

The sheriff scratched his head. "Hard to tell exactly what time old Giles fell into the pond. A drowned body doesn't get bloated right away," he said cheerfully. "Takes maybe a couple of days."

"Was there anything else you wanted to ask us, Sheriff?" Jason's voice sounded impatient, as if anxious to get the questioning over with.

"Suppose not. Seems pretty clear what happened. I'll talk some more to the hands, not that I reckon they'll have much to say."

He asked if Giles had any relatives to be notified and Jason said as far as he knew there were none. He would see that Giles received a decent burial.

Supper that night was a subdued affair. No one at the table did more than play with the delicious baked ham, swimming in Madeira sauce with thick slices of candied sweet potatoes. Even Quentin was quiet, his eyes red from crying. He sniffed occasionally, as if tears were still close to the surface.

Finally, after one particularly loud sniff, Jason said irritably,

"Either blow your nose, Quentin, or leave the table. You're certainly old enough to know how to use your handkerchief properly."

Charlotte gave Jason an outraged glance, then putting her arm around the boy, whispered to him. He excused himself and left the table. As soon as he was gone, Charlotte turned upon Jason indignantly, "There's no need to scold the boy, Jason. Naturally he's upset over Giles's death. We all are."

A scornful glint appeared in Jason's eyes as his glance traveled around the table. "So you're upset, are you? That's strange, considering that only last night you all seemed convinced that Giles was some sort of monster who should be thown out of Fernwood."

There was an awkward silence which Rowena finally broke by turning to me curiously. "Why did you ask the sheriff how long Giles's body had been in the water, Abigail?"

I shifted in my chair uncomfortably, wondering if it would be better not to say anything. Still, perhaps I wasn't the only one in the household who had heard the drunken singing. "Last night, I was awakened by someone singing. I thought it might be Giles."

Charlotte thought a moment then shook her head. "I didn't hear anything, but if you did, it was probably Jonas you heard. He often gets into the cooking sherry if Dulcy doesn't watch him."

"What difference does it make if it was Giles?" Rob asked.

I spoke slowly, feeling my way. "Well, if it was Giles I heard, then he must have returned to his room last night, and then gone back to the pond later. But why should he do that? Unless he didn't fall off the bridge last night at all but on his way to the fields this morning." I frowned unhappily. "Only he wouldn't still be drunk by then, would he? And he would hardly have fallen off the bridge if he were sober."

"What exactly are you trying to say, Abigail?" Jason's voice was biting.

I wished now that I hadn't spoken at all. Only again, wasn't it too much of a coincidence that the very night that Jason agreed to question Giles about Celia's death was the same night that Giles should stumble to his death in the ice pond?

Rob gave me an amused glance. "I think what Abigail is saying is that she believes someone deliberately pushed old Giles into the pond. Isn't that what you're saying, Abigail?"

CHAPTER SIXTEEN

"That's enough, Rob!" Jason's chair screeched protestingly as he pushed it back over the polished floor. His face stained a dark, angry red. "Miss Prentice is obviously not herself. Her accident, and now finding Giles's body, has been a great strain. Perhaps, Abigail, you would like to retire to your room."

I stared at him, speechless. He was sending me from the table the way he had Quentin, as if I were a child who had misbehaved. It was impossible to believe those eyes had ever looked at me with tenderness, with yearning. It was the face of a stranger, a man I didn't know, had never known. I stumbled to my feet, murmuring something, I would never know what, and found myself outdoors in the garden, rubbing my hands up and down my arms as if to warm myself.

It was there that Rob found me later, his voice apologetic, "I'm sorry, Abby. Jason had no right to behave in such a high-handed fashion."

"Why not?" I asked curtly. "Don't you agree with Jason, that I'm imagining things about Giles's death, the way I imagined seeing the cavalier in the garden?"

Rob plucked a rose leaf and shredded it thoughtfully. "Oh, I don't doubt that someone could have pushed old Giles off the bridge. There are plenty of ex-slaves within fifty miles of Fernwood who hated him enough to want him dead."

That thought hadn't occurred to me, that some field worker Giles had mistreated in the old days could have lain in wait at the bridge for the plantation overseer and exacted his revenge.

"Frankly it doesn't matter to me how Giles ended up in the pond," Rob said cheerfully. "I agree with Charlotte. He always acted a cut above himself. I never did understand why Jason kept him on. Unless . . ." He fell silent.

"Unless what?" I pressed.

"Nothing," he said quickly. "Let it drop, Abigail. Forget about Giles. I'm more concerned about you. I told you once, Jason is the wrong man to cross. I don't want to see you hurt."

Hadn't Giles warned me of the same thing, I remembered. That if I kept poking into matters that were none of my concern, I might find more than I bargained for. I might end up like Celia. I steadied my voice to hide the fear that chilled me. "Your brother needn't worry. I'll be leaving Fernwood tomorrow."

I was startled when Rob's hands suddenly grasped mine, his voice imploring urgently, "You mustn't leave, Abby. Not yet."

Embarrassed, I tried to draw my hands free. "Of course, I can't stay, Rob. How can I? Jason obviously doesn't want me here."

"Damn Jason!" Rob's voice was low, furious. "He may run Fernwood. He doesn't run me. And I want you to stay." Then smiling coaxingly, "Besides, Quentin will be desolate if you go. And so will I. In any case, your leg's not strong enough yet for you to travel alone. Give yourself a few days, at least."

This time I did remove my hands, my thoughts uncertain. There was no question of my remaining at Fernwood. It would only be embarrassing, both for Jason and me. But it was equally true that my leg still bothered me, and would make traveling uncomfortable.

"Please, Abby, what can a few days matter?" Rob insisted. "For my sake, promise me you'll stay until you're sure you're completely recovered."

I felt myself wavering. There was no doubting the concern in Rob's voice and it was comforting to my bruised vanity, I had to admit, to have someone interested in my welfare. "I don't know, Rob," I said slowly. "I'll have to think about it."

As I returned to my room, climbing with difficulty up the steep veranda staircase, I thought I smelled cigar smoke on the upstairs veranda. Had Jason stood here, I wondered uneasily, watching Rob and me together in the garden? Did he care at all, I thought, as I undressed for bed. Had Jason ever cared really, or had it been a pretense from the minute he had read the letter from my aunt's lawyers telling him that I was a wealthy heiress. And he saw a way out of Fernwood's financial problems.

I was sure I had completely accepted the fact of Jason's betrayal. Now as pain flicked through my body, I realized that only my mind had accepted it. My emotions were still raw, still aching without the protective scar tissue that time would bring.

The next morning was Giles's funeral. I wasn't invited and I had no desire to attend anyway. When the family returned, Mrs. Barclay immediately retired to her room. Rowena whispered to me that her aunt was suffering from "one of her spells of rheumatism."

I taught the boys their lessons and under other conditions, I would have been gratified at Quentin's pathetic eagerness to please me. At the end of the lesson, he lingered, asking anxiously, "Uncle Rob says you'll be leaving Fernwood, Miss Prentice. You won't, will you?"

"I'm afraid I must, Quentin."

The boy gazed furtively around him, as if to make sure he wasn't overheard. "Do you think the cavalier's gone now?" he whispered. "After you leave, do you think he'll come back?"

Wryly I realized that it wasn't so much affection for me that made Quentin want me to stay. I was his bulwark against the cavalier's wrath, the only one who believed his story.

"I'm sure he's gone, Quentin," I said gently. "You mustn't worry. Besides you have your uncles to look after you."

The boy's voice grew bitter. "I don't! Uncle Rob always goes away and Uncle Jason, he doesn't even like me."

"That's not true," I protested, hoping my voice carried more conviction than I felt. "Your Uncle Jason loves you very much."

The boy pulled free of my grasp, his face contorted with childish anger. "That's a lie. No one likes me. Even Aunt Charlotte . . . I heard her crying last night. When I wanted to go into her room, her door was locked. Well, I'll show them. I'll show them all."

He darted away. Si hesitated, giving me an anxious glance. "Go after him, Si," I said, worried. "He needs you."

The boy nodded soberly and ran after Quentin.

That evening I accepted Rob's invitation to stroll in the garden because I wanted to talk to him about my concern for Quentin, but he was impatient to talk of other matters. "I've written a friend of mine in Boston, Abby," he said eagerly. "We met at White Sulphur Springs last year. I did him a favor then, and I'm sure when we arrive in Boston, we can stay with his family until we can find suitable living quarters for you."

"We?" I asked, startled. "You're coming to Boston?"

"Of course," he said, as if surprised I should ask. "You don't think I'd let you travel that distance alone. And once you reach Boston, you'll need someone to look after you."

"I'm quite capable of looking after myself."

"That was before, Abigail," he said gravely. "You don't seem to realize, you're a woman of considerable fortune now. There'll be all sorts of unscrupulous people, waiting to prey upon a young, unprotected female in your position."

"You mean men who'll want to marry me for my money," I said.

In the moonlight, I saw Rob flinch and I turned away, embarrassed. "I'm sorry, Rob," I murmured. "I shouldn't have said that."

"Forget Jason," he ordered. His hand fastened on my waist, forced me gently around to face him. "Don't turn away from me, Abigail. Look at me. Remember that night in the drawing room? I haven't forgotten. I don't think you have either." At the last minute before his lips found mine, I tried to pull free. But it was too late.

It wasn't like the first time he kissed me. I felt no sensation of shock. I felt nothing at all.

When he released me and stepped back, his handsome face looked as if it were etched in silver in the moonlight. "So it's still Jason," he said, his voice oddly flat.

"No, of course not," I stammered. "It's just that it's late, Rob, and I'm tired."

I retreated as gracefully and as quickly as my leg would allow me. At the foot of the veranda stairs, I thought I heard Rob behind me. But when I turned and looked back, he was still standing where I left him, staring after me.

I inched my way up the veranda stairs, holding tightly to the balustrade. My cheeks felt flushed and I was glad for the darkness that hid my face when I reached the top step. For Jason stood waiting for me. In the darkness, he loomed suddenly before me like a boulder blocking my path.

I stopped short. "I didn't know you were here."

"Obviously," he commented drily. "It's plain your eyes have been elsewhere lately."

So he had been standing here on the veranda, watching Rob and me in the garden, I thought, and was irritated at the guilt I felt. After all, it was no longer any business of his how I occupied my time. "I don't know what you're talking about, and now if you'll excuse me . . ."

He did not move. To reach the French doors of the little sitting room, I would have to walk around him. As I started to do so, his hand caught my wrist so tightly that I winced.

"It won't work, Abigail," he said. "You haven't the talent or the experience for this sort of game. Your face is too open. It gives you away."

I struggled to free my hand. "You don't know what you're saying!" I caught the odor of whiskey on his breath. The more I struggled, the tighter the hold on my wrist became.

"You might say I've been through all this before," he said, smiling coldly. "Now Celia could lie in my arms, her face like an angel, and all the time it was Brian she was imagining holding her. Are you experienced enough to do that, my love? To kiss me and imagine I'm Rob?"

"Let me go!"

His other arm slipped around my waist in a vise. "I suppose you find him charming. It's amazing how boyish charm and a pretty face can addle a woman's brain."

"At least Rob has never pretended with me," I said, furious now. "He's never lied to me."

"No?" Jason laughed mockingly. "Then ask him about his life in Richmond, his gambling debts, the women he's loved and left. When your money's gone, you'll see how quickly his ardor cools."

"That's not true!" Only somewhere deep inside of me, some fragment of common sense still left to me told me it was true. It wasn't any beauty or charm on my part that had aroused Rob's interest in me. It was my inheritance. The humiliation of that knowledge sent a shock wave of anger through me. I wanted to hurt Jason as much as he had hurt me.

"What does it matter? The money Aunt Agnes left me almost bought me a husband. Why shouldn't it buy me a lover?"

The arm around my waist tightened like a loop of iron so that the breath left my body. If I hadn't been so appalled at what I had just said, I would have been frightened at the slate coldness of Jason's face, the dazed fury in his eyes staring down at me, as if he were not seeing me at all but someone else, another time, another place—another woman, struggling furiously in his arms. There was nothing gentle about that embrace. It was sheer, massive force trying to compel a response, using his strength pitilessly so that I could no longer struggle but felt myself helplessly being pulled into the vortex of the storm. I think I managed once to cry out, for suddenly the arms released me. I stumbled backward, came up hard against the brick wall by the French door.

"Do you really think I'd let you go to him?" I flinched at the contempt in his voice. "Do you think I'd allow any woman to make a fool of me? You should know by now that I don't give up easily what's mine."

All at once I understood. "Did Celia want to be set free?" I whispered.

He took a sharp breath and the rage drained from his eyes, leaving only a pain so intense that it must never be acknowledged or it could not be endured.

Swaying, he stood to one side. "As long as we understand each other. Good night, Abigail."

He allowed me to walk by him, through the sitting room, and

into the bedroom. Once in the blue bedroom, I heard him enter the sitting room and close the bedroom door behind me. Then to my surprise, a second later, I heard the sharp, metallic sound of sliding metal. The door from my bedroom to the sitting room had been locked from the outside.

I stared at the door, stunned. Then turned and hurried to the other door that led into the upstairs hallway. Almost before I touched the knob, I knew. That door was locked, too.

CHAPTER SEVENTEEN

At first, I couldn't believe it. I tried the door a second time. There was no mistake. The door was locked. I was a prisoner in my own bedroom.

For a moment I debated beating at the door with my fists, demanding my release. But that would mean making a scene, facing Jason again. And the truth was I did not have the courage, not so soon after our last encounter. I undressed quickly and climbed into bed. After my tiny bed in the sitting room, the black walnut bed seemed an enormous plain, a great empty expanse reaching around me, the dark blue canopy overhead like a too low ceiling pressing down upon me. Purple hued shadows crouched in the corners of the room, held at bay by the orange glow of the lamp I kept burning dimly beside the bed. Not for anything would I have extinguished the lamp. This time I knew for sure the scent of roses was from the bouquet beside the bed but I was taking no chances. If Celia still claimed this room as her own, at least we wouldn't share it in the dark!

Whatever fear I felt, however, was overshadowed by my anger at Jason's domineering treatment of me. As if I were one of his helpless, male-dominated, Southern women, I thought grimly. Well, he would find out differently in the morning.

When I awoke the next morning, memory returned in a rush, propelling me out of bed and to the hall door. The knob turned easily beneath my hand.

Had I imagined the door was locked last night, I wondered. No, it had happened, just as my conversation with Jason had happened. I felt a tingle of shame, remembering how childishly spiteful I had been, flinging the lie that I was Rob's mistress in Jason's face.

Still, that was no excuse for the way Jason had spoken to me, the cruel strength in his hands, holding me. No, not me, I thought slowly. It was Celia that Jason had been seeing, holding in his arms last night. What had happened between them those hours before Jason rode off to the bachelor's party? Had my wild guess last night been right? Had Celia at the last minute asked Jason to release her from their engagement so she could go off with Brian, and Jason, furious, had refused to let her go? Refused to allow a woman to jilt him the night before their wedding and make him the laughing stock of the county.

Only I doubted if Celia was a woman to be intimidated easily. Suppose what Rob had suggested to me in the drawing room had actually happened, Jason returning early from the party and surprising his fiancée in the act of running off with his brother. What would Jason have done then? But I didn't want to think about that and I hastily pushed the thought away. Anyway, Celia hadn't been planning on leaving Jason. She had died, if not peacefully, at least in her nightgown in bed.

I finished dressing and hurried down to breakfast. Almost as soon as I entered the dining room, I sensed that something was wrong. Jason wasn't there but I didn't expect him to be. He always ate earlier than anyone else in the house and with Giles gone, his work day would begin even sooner. Only Rowena and Charlotte, with Quentin beside her, sat at the table.

Rowena glanced up nervously when I entered, then back at her plate. It was Quentin who piped up eagerly, "Uncle Rob and Uncle Jason had a fight!"

"Quentin!" Mrs. Barclay pressed the boy's arm, trying to silence him.

"Well, they did," the boy insisted. "I heard Jonas tell Dulcy that Uncle Jason sent Uncle Rob packing." He gazed at me curiously. "Did you hear them fighting, Miss Prentice?"

"No." I slipped uneasily into my chair. "No, I didn't."

"Neither did I," Quentin said, disappointed, and then, apparently fascinated at the thought, "Do you suppose if Uncle Jason had a gun he would have shot Uncle Rob?"

His aunt said sharply: "If you've finished your breakfast, you're excused, Quentin."

Quentin started to protest but something about the chalky whiteness of his aunt's face made him change his mind. Obediently he slipped out of his chair and ran from the room, shouting for Si.

I glanced bewildered at Mrs. Barclay. "I don't understand. Where did Rob go?"

She shrugged her narrow shoulders. "I believe he's staying with the Jensons at Twin Oaks for a few days, until . . . until his plans are more settled."

With a quick, unhappy glance toward her aunt, Rowena handed me a letter across the table. "Rob asked me to give this to you."

The note was hastily scribbled in Rob's handwriting: *Jason has made it clear that I must leave Fernwood at once. Rather than cause the family embarrassment, I have agreed. However, I will not be far away from you. If you need me, send word through the Jensons and I will come at once. Love, Rob.*

I flushed, annoyed, and got to my feet. "I'll speak to Jason," I said. "He can't allow . . ."

Charlotte interrupted acidly. "It'd be better if you didn't, Miss Prentice. Don't you think you've done enough harm?"

I didn't bother to argue. I had already learned it was like battling cobwebs, arguing with Charlotte Barclay. My leg was bothering me too much to walk to the fields so I limped to the stable and asked the stableboy to saddle my mare for me.

He gazed up at me, frightened, then down at his feet, mumbling, "I can't, Miss Abigail. Mr. Jason, he gave strict orders. No horses was to leave the stable less'n he says so."

The wave of anger that swept over me made me feel giddy as if I had had too much sun. "I see." My voice trembled. "Would you fetch me my cane then? I left it in the front hall."

Even with the help of the cane Jonas had devised for me, it took me half an hour to walk down the road to the tobacco field, stopping every few minutes to rest my leg. It took another ten minutes to locate Jason. The cutting of the tobacco was well under way. As I watched, I saw Jason at the end of a row take his pruning knife and with one sure movement slash a ripe stalk almost to the ground. The knife made a rending sound as if it were ripping flesh. The stalk trembled a moment then fell to join the others, piled at Jason's feet.

The juicy stubble left standing looked as if it were bleeding. The smell of tobacco hung, heavy, sickeningly sweet in the air around me. Jason turned to attack another stalk, the knife lifting and falling with the same ruthless rhythm. He had stripped off his jacket and I could see the powerful muscles in his back and shoulders straining beneath the cotton shirt. The brooding, intent look on his face shaded off into something akin to savagery.

When he turned toward me, a mask of composure settled over his face, glazed with sweat. I had meant to plead my case for Rob calmly, rationally, to make Jason understand how mistaken he was, but instead, infuriated by that blank mask, I blurted, "You can't keep me prisoner here, you know."

Jason gazed out over the field of tobacco as if his mind were on more important matters. "I can," he said indifferently, "for a few days. Until the fever subsides. That's one thing I've noticed about Rob's effect on young ladies. Like gardenias, the fragrance fades very quickly. Now if you'll excuse me, Abigail . . ."

I stared, frustrated, at the broad back he turned to me as he once more bent to the task of slicing and cutting. With no way to continue the conversation, I was forced to return to the house, arriving irritable and exhausted, my leg paining me from the exertion of the walk. Quentin and Si had arrived for their lessons, both of them curious as to what was going on, but I cut off their questions so sharply that even Quentin looked subdued.

I spent the rest of the day debating with myself how best I could leave Fernwood. I could go into the town of Crossroads but even with the short cut through the woods, that was at least a mile away and how would I reach there, without transportation? Perhaps I could persuade one of the servants to get word to Rob, but I hated involving him further in my personal problems. No matter how annoyed I was with Jason, I didn't want to drive a further wedge between him and his brother.

The evening meal that night was an awkward affair with Rob's chair glaringly empty. Quentin must have been warned not to say anything for he kept unusually quiet. Jason had the whiskey demijohn at the table beside him, and drank steadily. Although twice Mrs. Charlotte stared at him disapprovingly, she said nothing. Of us all, only Rowena seemed livelier than usual, her color high in her cheeks, her eyes bright. I wondered absently if she was the sort of person who thrived on the unhappiness of others, feeding a need within her that she couldn't fulfill any other way.

After dinner, Mrs. Barclay excused herself and went to her room, Quentin reluctantly in tow. Rowena stayed, I suppose hopefully to see if anything new transpired between Jason and me. Immediately Jason went off into the library to work on his books and since I wasn't in the mood to make conversation, Rowena, too, gave up and went to bed.

I strolled into the library and, finding a book, deliberately sat down and began reading. I was determined not to go to my bedroom first. No matter what Jason thought I would not be locked into my room again if I had to spend the whole night in the library.

Finally, after an hour, Jason yawned and got to his feet. "Will you be staying up much longer?" he asked.

My hand tightened on my book, my voice frigid. "You needn't worry, Jason. I don't plan to run away during the night."

He had the grace to look embarrassed then shrugged. "Very well. I'll see you in the morning then."

The door closed quietly behind him. Silence descended over the library except for my turning a page in the book that I forced myself to keep reading. The silence was almost too deep. It intruded upon my consciousness. Finally I gave up all pretense of reading. It was foolish to remain down here any longer. Surely by now Jason was asleep.

I replaced the book on the shelf and extinguished the lamps except for the one I carried with me to light my way up the stairs. I had reached the foot of the stairs when I stopped, startled. I could swear I heard the piano being played in the drawing room.

I hesitated a moment, then walked closer toward the great drawing-room doors. They stood open and I could hear the music more clearly now, a plaintive, familiar melody. *Londonderry Air*. Then all at once whoever was at the piano stopped playing. The deep silence made my own breathing sound loud. I heard the ordinary night sounds the house always made, the whir of the clock from the upstairs hall, the creak of a floor board settling. Ordinary, comforting sounds.

Then the music began again, softly, airily tripping through the darkness toward me as I stepped inside the drawing room. Charlotte? Rowena? Yet why should either of them sneak down in the middle of the night to play the piano?

I took a few more cautious steps inside the room, my lamp flinging a safe circle of light around me. The drapes in the room were all drawn except for the window at the far end of the room by the fireplace. Through that window, a gray shrouded moonlight drifted like mist, touching the base of the pilastered fireplace, the twin Windsor chairs, the piano. And the dark, tall figure with its back to me seated at the piano. Too tall for Charlotte.

"Rowena?" I asked hesitantly. The sound of my own voice lent me courage. "Is that you, Rowena?" I asked more loudly.

The music ended abruptly in the middle of a chord. The dancing notes hung suspended in the air before falling away into bottomless silence.

Then slowly the pianist rose and turned toward me. Now I knew why the figure had seemed unusually tall. It was the plumed hat shadowing its face, the long blue velvet cape. The moonlight swirled around the body of the cavalier so that it seemed ephemeral, as if it were not so much rooted to the floor but part of the shifting, mistlike moonlight, itself.

Then the moonlight remained and the cavalier simply disappeared before my eyes. No, not disappeared, I realized, clutching my lamp to me. Through the darkness, I could hear the sound of footsteps, a faint slither across the parquet floor, coming toward me. The darkness washed toward me and over me, bringing back memory of the nightmare in the garden, the same noisome horror possessed me now, the taste of fear acrid in my mouth.

I whirled and reached for the door behind me. Too quickly. My right leg twisted painfully beneath me, gave way, and I felt myself falling. Flinging out my arms to regain my balance, the lamp struck something solid in the darkness and crashed to the floor. The flame hissed, then was gone. In the thick blanket of darkness that instantly wrapped around my face, I lost all sense of reason, of direction. My hands reached out, searching frantically for the open door. It must be here. My fingers scratched at solid wood paneling. I began to whimper with fear, beating at the paneling with my clenched fist. Oh, God, where was the door?

I don't know how long I flung myself at the wall, probably not more than a few seconds, an eternity. Before I suddenly realized the slithering sound behind me had stopped.

Once more the room was caught in a deep, stagnant quiet. I turned slowly. Whatever had been in the room with me was gone. I knew it as surely as I was standing there. With hands that shook, I found the lamp on the floor. After three tries I managed to relight it. Then I moved slowly forward, the light spilling ahead of me down the long room, touched the piano bench. There was no one there.

I walked past the row of windows, checking each one as I went but each window was shut and locked from the inside. I threw my lamplight behind the drapes. Nothing. As if the cavalier had melted into the darkness.

The fear that shook me then was much worse than before, shattering my self-control. At least, the cavalier in the garden had been real, visible. Something with human form and shape. A reality I could cope with. Not this shapeless evil that I had experienced here in the drawing room, a darkness that threatened to possess me, pull me into its grasp. A scream rose in my throat and I choked it back, gagging with the effort. All I knew was that I must hurry, hurry . . . leave this place before I was lost completely.

I half fell up the staircase, pulled myself to my feet, would have crawled if necessary to reach the safety of my bedroom. Once there I locked both doors, pulled the drapes across the window, then sank into a chair. My body felt like a chunk of ice. I rubbed my hands together and began to tremble violently as if my very bones would be shaken apart. The knifelike thrusts of pain in my right hip and thigh became a dull, agonizing throbbing.

It was pain that drove me to my feet and into the sitting room to find the bottle of laudanum the doctor had left with me. I took one teaspoon, then a second, forced myself not to think about anything but getting undressed, crawling into bed, pulling the comforter over me and still feeling cold. As if I would never be warm again.

The cold was the last thing I remembered before the laudanum took hold and I drifted off into a merciful, drugged sleep.

CHAPTER EIGHTEEN

It was the sound of someone knocking at my door that finally aroused me the next morning. I struggled up from sleep like fighting my way through a thick gray fog.

Dulcy stood in the doorway with a tray of food in her hands. "Miss Rowena was worried, you didn't come down for breakfast." Then, with a sharp glance at my face, "Are you feeling poorly, Miss Prentice?"

I managed to sit up, memory slowly sifting back. Was it real what had happened in the drawing room last night, I wondered, confused. Or was it only the same nightmare, the cavalier pursuing me then disappearing like a wisp of smoke. I shook my head drowsily, "I'm all right, Dulcy. I just overslept."

"I brought you breakfast." I saw slices of ham and eggs swimming in golden butter. My stomach turned over and I looked away.

"Thank you, Dulcy, I'm not hungry. Coffee will be fine."

She came into the room quickly, looking neither to the right nor left. After she placed the tray on a table and poured the coffee, she withdrew again to the door, as if not wanting to stay in the room a moment longer than was necessary. I remembered then and asked, "You found her, didn't you, Dulcy?"

She didn't pretend not to know what I meant. She folded her hands together beneath her white apron, her voice stolid. "Yes'm, there on the bed. The curtains was drawn. At first, I thought she was asleep. Until I saw her head on the pillow, covered with blood."

I clutched the carved post of the bed, gazing into those dark opaque eyes. "You didn't like her, did you, Dulcy?"

She shrugged. "I never thought on it."

"Was she . . . unkind to you, Dulcy?"

She shook her head. "Mostly she stayed clear of the servants. She said she didn't like them touching her. I s'pose, being foreign, she wasn't used to being around colored folks."

"I've been told she was very beautiful."

Dulcy's eyes suddenly flared fire, her face filled with a primordial wrath. "Lucifer's beautiful when he tempts you with his sweet words and coaxin' ways. But the good Lord smites the devil down."

I spoke carefully, hoping to keep her talking. "You don't believe she shot herself, do you, Dulcy?"

But the black face was once again carefully blank, the eyes shuttered. "I don't think on matters that don't concern me. You shouldn't either, Miss Abigail." Then in a low voice, speaking in a rush as if afraid she might change her mind. "Go back to your own people, child. You don't belong here at the hall. It's not safe."

"Why, Dulcy? Why isn't it safe?"

In my eagerness I slipped to my feet, walked toward the woman, but she fell back, as if she was sorry now she had spoken. She shook her head helplessly. "You've been good to my Si. I'm not forgetting that, but there's only sorrow for you here. Sorrow and death . . . like her . . ." She gestured toward the bed and then in one swift movement she turned and left me, staring after her.

I took my coffee cup and walked through the sitting room out onto the veranda. It was a hot morning, the air close and humid, with layers of clouds like dirty gray blankets pressing down upon the earth. The moonflower vine hung limp and the mimosa leaves turned inward, like tiny, clenched hands. In the tobacco fields most of the plants had been cut. The fields had the struck down look of a battlefield.

It wasn't the fields I was seeing though. I was reliving moment by moment what had happened in the drawing room the night before. It was all so real, so vivid in my mind. Was it possible I could have imagined it all, the piano music, the ghostly figure that had vanished before my eyes. I remembered my father telling me of a young brilliant doctor in Vienna who was discovering amazing insights into the human brain, the strange, frightening tricks the mind plays on itself. Was that what was happening to me? Was I losing my mind?

No! I began to pace back and forth, determinedly ignoring the twinges of pain in my leg. I wouldn't believe it. I mustn't believe it. If I started doubting my senses, believing in ghosts and hallucinations then I would finally begin to doubt what I had seen in the garden. The only thing I knew for sure was that this time it couldn't have been Giles impersonating the cavalier in the drawing room. Giles was as dead as Guy Barclay . . . as Celia . . .

Celia. Always, always it came back to Celia, I thought in despair. It was her shadow that hung over Fernwood. If anyone's shade stalked the halls of Fernwood, it was not the cavalier but his victim. It was Celia's presence I had always felt as a barrier between Jason and me, between Jason and Rob, as if even after death, she still had the power to split the Barclay family apart.

Somehow I was sure if I could unravel the tangled skein of Celia's death . . . I sighed and stopped to rest a moment in a wicker chair. Whatever chance I had of unmasking Celia's killer had died with Giles. Anyway, it was myself I should be concerned about, not Celia. How did I know the cavalier wouldn't appear to me again and the next time claim another victim, another "accidental" death? I had thought with Giles dead, I was safe. Now I wondered if I would ever be safe at Fernwood. Wasn't that what Dulcy had tried to warn me?

Pushing myself to my feet, I hurried into the bedroom. I had to find a way to leave Fernwood, today, before it was too late. I found my worn carpetbag in the wardrobe, pulled it out and packed with a feverish haste. There was little enough to pack. I hadn't brought many clothes with me to Fernwood. Finally I changed into my gray merino traveling gown, the one I had worn when I arrived. Looking around the room, with my few toilet articles removed, the wardrobe standing empty, it was as if I had never been in the room at all.

When the knock came at the door, I thought it was Dulcy returning for the breakfast tray and I called for her to come in. To my surprise, Jason came into the room. He was in his work clothes, but he held a silver tray with a glass of egg nog on it. "Dulcy told me you didn't eat any breakfast and I noticed you hardly touched your meal last night. You have to eat, Abigail, or you'll never get your strength back. Charlotte fixed you an egg nog. She thought it might tempt your appetite."

I started to say I wasn't hungry but it was plain that Jason was presenting the egg nog as a peace offering and that it was as difficult for him to make the gesture as it was for me to face him.

Obediently I swallowed a little of the drink then gave Jason a startled glance. He smiled sheepishly. "I laced it with rum. I thought it might help."

For a moment the smile hid the weariness that etched deep lines of exhaustion from his nose to his mouth, his eyes drained pale of all color. Looking at him, I suddenly knew how Jason would look when he was old and my heart wrenched with pity, or was it love. I was no longer sure. All I knew was that we mustn't part like this, like enemies. I reached out my hand. "Jason, I'm sorry . . ."

Then for the first time he noticed the empty wardrobe, the carpetbag at my feet and his voice stiffened. "So you're going to Rob."

My hand fell. Wearily I shook my head. "No, I'm not going to Rob. But you must see that I can't stay on here at Fernwood. Please, Jason, don't make it any harder for me. Let me go."

He stood a moment, gazing at me, without speaking. Then to my surprise, he shrugged, almost indifferently. "Very well, if that's what you want. I suppose I was wrong to try and keep you here. You'll have to wait till Jonas returns though. He took the carriage and drove the family into town. As soon as he comes back, I'll have him take you to the stagecoach stop."

I tried to read his eyes. Was there sadness there, regret? I only knew he had come to a decision and whatever had been between us, was finished. My eyes blurred and I turned away so he wouldn't see the tears. "Goodbye, Jason," I said. And heard the door close quietly behind him.

I wondered how long it would be before Jonas returned from town, at least two or three hours. I felt restless and taking the egg nog, walked carefully down the veranda steps for a last stroll through the garden. Despite the hollow ache in my chest, I discovered I was hungry and had just finished the egg nog when Si came toward me from the stable, his voice regretful. "I reckon with Marse Quentin in town, we won't have a lesson today."

I smiled at the boy's eagerness, thinking that here was another regret I would take with me. Who would bother teaching Si after I left? What would happen to that eager, untrained mind then? Perhaps, I thought suddenly, I could take some of Aunt Agnes' money and send it to Dulcy, make sure she sent Si to school. There was a good school for black children that had been started recently in Boston by friends of my father.

I sat down on a bench and explained, "I'm sorry I won't be able to teach you any longer, Si . . ." and then quickly, at the crestfallen look on the boy's face, "But I intend to see that you continue going to school after I leave Fernwood."

"Why do you have to go, Miss Abigail? Quentin and me, we like you teaching us." Then, anxiously, "Jonas says the cavalier put a hex on you that night in the garden. Is that why you're going?"

I shook my head. Although I couldn't help reflecting wryly that, unless I wanted to start believing in ghosts, someone at Fernwood was putting a hex on me, trying to frighten me out of my wits, to drive me away. Why else the piano playing in the drawing room, when everyone else had gone to bed, except me, the only one who would hear it . . .

I frowned and sat up straighter. The piano playing *Londonderry Air* hadn't been executed very skillfully but it had been played by a human hand. Still that wasn't much help. Mrs. Barclay had said that all the young Barclays had been taught a little about the piano, even Rob and Jason. No doubt she and Rowena played a little, too.

Yet it was a beginning. As for the rest, the dark-caped figure in the moonlight suddenly vanishing. All he had to do was step outside the pool of moonlight into the darkness and he would seem to disappear. What wasn't humanly possible was that he could have left the drawing room without my noticing. I had checked the locks on the windows and he couldn't have passed me at the hall door. There hadn't been time.

Si tugged timidly at my skirt. "You feeling all right, Miss Abigail? You want me to fetch you some water?"

"No, I was thinking, Si. A puzzle that I can't figure out." And then on an impulse. "Would you like to hear it?"

"You mean lak a riddle?"

"Sort of like a riddle," I agreed. "Suppose you were in the drawing room and you weren't supposed to be there, like that night I found you in the library. And suppose someone came into the drawing room. How would you get away?"

"I'd jump out those fancy windows!"

"No, the windows are locked and the person would hear you opening them and catch you before you got away."

Si pursed his lips thoughtfully. Then he said triumphantly, "I'd hide in the closet. That's what I'd do."

"There aren't any closets in the drawing room," I reminded him.

Si reached for my hand. "Yes, there is a closet. I'll show you."

He almost dragged me through the hallway into the drawing room. Halfway down the room, I paused to rest my leg, asking, "Si, wait, where are we going?"

He danced ahead of me toward the far end of the room where a wall of paneling reached to the ceiling on either side of the pillared fireplace. A crystal candlesconce was hung in the center of each panel. I watched as Si ran his hand expertly along the base of the paneling, finally found what he was seeking and pressed.

Without making a sound, the paneling swung quietly open.

Si laughed with excitement at my surprise. "It's a hidey hole," he chortled. "Granny Dulcy told me about it. When the Yankees came, this is where old Mrs. Barclay hid her valuables."

I advanced slowly. When I got close enough, I could see the dust on the floor of the closet was disturbed, as if someone or something had stood there recently. The cavalier, I thought, my heart all at once pounding. The closet was large enough to hold a person. All the cavalier had to do was play the piano until I was lured into the dark drawing room. Then during my panic-stricken bolt for the door, he had simply slipped quietly into the closet, remained hidden until after I had left the room.

No doubt all the Barclays knew about the closet. Charlotte, Rowena, Jason. Any one of them could have crept into this room last night. Even Rob. No, Rob was at Twin Oaks last night, I reminded myself. Still, Twin Oaks wasn't that far away. He could have returned with no one knowing. Just as years before, I thought suddenly, he could have left the bachelor party at Silver Grove, returned to Fernwood. I frowned, exasperated. But why? Rob, of all people, would have no reason to want to frighten me. Any more than Rowena or Mrs. Charlotte had. And that left only Jason. A cramp all at once twisted inside of me, almost doubling me up with the pain. Not Jason . . . please, not Jason.

"Did I solve your riddle for you?" Si asked eagerly.

"Yes, you did, Si." My stomach churned as if I were going to be sick. I reached out a hand steadying myself on his thin, strong shoulder. "I'm going to my room now and rest. You'd better run home. It looks like it's going to rain."

"Yes'm." He gave me a last worried glance when we reached the foot of the stairs then he darted toward the back door.

Once in my room, I sat down a moment until the queasiness passed. But my feeling of restlessness, of excitement remained. All my senses: vision, taste, smell, felt curiously sharpened. When I lit the lamp against the gathering gloom of the storm, the light made me blink with pain, as if it were daggers jabbing at my eyes.

I found it impossible to sit quietly and began to prowl back and forth, my nerves pulled taut, my thoughts racing feverishly. I was not going mad, after all. There had been someone in the drawing room with me last night, not my imagination, not a hallucination, but flesh and blood, as real as the cavalier who had attacked me in the garden. Someone who was afraid I was getting too close to solving the mystery of Celia Rougier's death. What other reason could there be for the attempts to frighten, to kill me. Why else was I a danger to someone here at Fernwood?

My glance swung around the luxurious blue bedroom, Celia's bedroom, trying to see the room through her eyes, the way she must have seen it that last night before she died. Trying, as if I were shedding my own skin, to put myself in her place, inside her mind. I would be lying on that great bed in my white nightgown, my black hair loose upon the pillow. A Saratoga trunk stood where a worn carpetbag now stood. The empty wardrobe door would be half open so as not to crush my wedding gown, a froth of white, the wedding veil draped over a chair. Everything ready and waiting for my wedding in the morning, the honeymoon trip afterwards. Everything . . . except . . .

My eyes fastened, narrowing, on the wardrobe. Something wrong. Something out of place, like a blurred picture slowly coming into focus. Then suddenly I knew exactly what had bothered me about Rowena's description of Celia's room the morning they found her, what bothered me now about the empty wardrobe. *Where was Celia's traveling gown?*

Surely that should have been hanging somewhere in the room that morning if Celia was planning to leave Fernwood immediately after the wedding ceremony. But Rowena had said the only clothes in the wardrobe had been the wedding gown and a few housedresses, no suitable clothes even in which to bury Celia. Where had the traveling dress been then . . . unless . . . unless the dress was missing . . .

My thoughts darted ahead of me, questions leaping into my mind faster than I could answer them. Suppose the traveling dress was missing because Celia had been wearing it, not her nightgown, when she died. Suppose at the last minute, Brian had persuaded her to run away with him. Wouldn't she have slipped into her most useful gown, the traveling dress from her trousseau?

Yet it was all speculation. For all I knew the traveling dress might be packed innocently in that locked trunk in the attic. All at once I had to know. I would need a lamp, I thought, and something with which to pry open the lock.

I hurried as quickly as I could down the veranda stairs, through the garden to the kitchen. I did not see any servants but that didn't surprise me. Dulcy usually went into town with Rowena and whenever Rowena was away from Fernwood, the other servants always disappeared about their own business. I found a butcher's knife on a pantry shelf and hobbled back to the house, the dark gray sky arching like a stone vault over my head. In the distance, thunder grumbled. Streaks of white fire split the sky over the tobacco fields; the garden blazed in sudden brilliance.

When I mounted the attic steps and found the trunk, I was trembling so, I had to grasp both hands around the hilt, to steady the knife. It was useless to try and break open the padlock. The fastest way was to pry loose the brass hasp from the leather. I began to jab and tear at the dry brittle leather. The sharp ripping sounds of the knife against leather sounded unnaturally loud in my ears. I could hear my heart beat with each thrust of the knife, pounding in my ears. Perspiration flecked my face; the palms of my hand wet so I had to stop a moment and dry them on the skirt of my gown, before I began again, stabbing, gouging, through the leather, into the wood beneath. My hands lifting, falling, like an automaton, possessed of a strength I had never known before, until finally the hasp fell away, dropped crookedly, torn loose from the hinge.

I let the knife drop, leaned forward to lift the lid of the trunk. The scent of attar of roses, weak but still fragrant, wafted upward, a fragrance that seemed to bring Celia alive, as if she were standing beside me, urging me on. We were no longer strangers and rivals, Celia and I. Her fears, her loves, her loneliness were mine now. We understood each other.

Without hesitating, I lifted the green velvet traveling dress flung carelessly on top of the neatly piled clothes in the trunk, and for a moment felt a sharp shock of disappointment. So the gown was not missing after all.

Until I held the dress closer to the lamplight. Something stiff and flaking brushed my hand. And I saw the dark brown stains on the bodice of the green velvet, caked and ugly blotches that could only be blood. Celia's blood.

CHAPTER NINETEEN

The crushed velvet material of the gown clung to my hands, the emerald sheen glowing in the lamplight as if the gown had been packed away yesterday instead of a decade before. Absently I stroked the shimmering softness, knowing the truth now, the truth I had fought against all along, and wondering why I felt so little sense of shock, only a sort of numbness.

It was Jason who had killed Celia, not Brian. It was Jason who must have returned home unexpectedly early from the party and discovered Celia dressed in her traveling gown, preparing to leave him. Who else at Fernwood would have cared that the bride-to-be had changed her mind the night before her wedding? Rowena and Charlotte would be relieved that Celia would be finally gone from Fernwood. Guy and Rob, even if their emotions ran deeper than they should have for their brother's fiancée, they both knew they had no chance to win her. And Brian. Why should Brian kill his love? He had won the prize. Only Jason was the loser. Jason was losing the only woman he had ever loved.

Then through my numbness, horror seeped like icy water through a crevice. Not just horror at Celia's death but what must have come afterwards. After he had shot Celia, the urgent necessity for Jason to remove the incriminating traveling gown. What had he felt then, I wondered, after the first blinding rage had passed . . . as his hands fumbled with buttons and ribbons, tearing off the bloodstained velvet garment, the chemise and petticoats from that white body, and finally pulling over the unresistant shoulders a frilly, pristine white nightgown that would be immediately stained red with blood.

Panic certainly. The traveling dress must be disposed of and quickly, the velvet gown that pointed out so clearly that Celia had been dressed to leave Fernwood, to leave Jason.

Her trunk was packed and ready for the next day's departure. How easy it must have seemed to Jason to shove the bloodstained clothes into the trunk, lock the trunk and pocket the key. Undoubtedly he planned to return after the excitement died down and quietly remove and destroy the bloodstained gown. Even that turned out to be unnecessary. Guy had ordered the trunk burned and it had been as far as Jason knew. Only he hadn't counted upon Charlotte's frugal nature.

I stumbled to my feet, clutching the gown in one hand, the lamp in the other. Thunder crashed against the rooftop, shaking the house. The attic windows were black; the storm was directly overhead now. The feeling of giddy, unnatural excitement had left me, drained away without my noticing. I felt depleted of all emotion. All I wanted to do was return to my room, lay my head down on the bed and sink into the oblivion of sleep.

When I reached my room, though, I knew there was no time for sleep. If I were to leave Fernwood, it would have to be now, while Jason was safely out in the fields and the house deserted. I couldn't take the chance of facing Jason again. I didn't have his talent for lying, for dissembling. He would see the truth in my eyes. And how could I predict what he would do then?

I would saddle my mare and ride to Twin Oaks, I decided. Rob was there. He would help me, tell me what to do. I picked up my shawl, surprised at how heavy it felt in my hands. It was an effort to place it around my shoulders. I did not even attempt to carry my satchel. I would send for my clothes later, I thought, crossing the sitting room and stepping out onto the veranda. And almost fell forward as the wind struck me in the back like a giant, playful hand, thrusting me down the veranda stairs, along the path to the stable, as if I were as weightless as a leaf.

Once inside the shelter of the stable, I rested a moment, leaning against the wall, catching my breath. Then I found the lamp and lit it. In his stall, Firefly tossed his head, unnerved by the storm, his hoofs striking at the wooden barrier of his stall, red pinpoints of terror in his eyes. My mare, Mary-belle, simply stared at me placidly.

As I crossed the expanse of the stable, I suddenly had the sensation that all this had happened to me before. No, not to me, to Celia, as if I had slipped inside her skin, was reliving her life. Yes, here was where it had happened, I thought, shivering, not in the elegant blue bedroom but here in the stable Celia had died. I knew it as surely as if I had stood by and watched it happen.

But Celia's death no longer mattered. Nothing mattered now except the frantic feeling possessing me, urging me to hurry faster, as my hands fumbled with the unfamiliar task of saddling the mare. When the stable door banged open behind me, I thought at first it was the wind, until I heard footsteps crossing the stable floor, felt a hand tighten on my shoulder, inexorably forcing me to turn around and face him.

I stared into the furious blue eyes, at the features, like chiseled stone, at the solid bulk of his body braced like a wall before me.

"Where do you think you're going?" he demanded angrily.

"I . . . I thought you were in the fields."

"Si fetched me. He said you were ill."

A few minutes, I thought despairingly, only a few more minutes and I would have mounted Marybelle and rode away from Fernwood for good, escaped Jason completely. Only a few minutes . . .

I discovered to my dismay that I was crying. I could taste the saltiness of tears on my lips as I cried helplessly, "You can't make me stay here. I will go away. I will! I found Celia's traveling gown, saw the blood on it. I know now. Don't you see, I know . . ."

Jason's face blurred before my eyes, even his voice, calmer now, without any hint of emotion, seemed to be coming from a great distance. "Be quiet, Abigail. Don't say any more. You're sick. I'll carry you back to your room. You'll feel better there."

"No . . . no! Let me go."

When his hands moved to lift me, I struggled to free myself, beating at his chest with my fists. Somehow I knew once I was back in that blue bedroom, I was lost. I would never escape him again. But, of course, my resistance was useless, like throwing pebbles at a stone wall. His arms circled, lifted me easily, my face buried against his chest.

His voice murmured, almost tenderly, "I can't let you go, my love. You know that."

Then we were through the garden, past the kitchen, going up the veranda stairs. Jason had to shift me awkwardly in his arms on that narrow staircase. The way he must have carried Celia, I thought, a dead weight in his arms. Dead . . . but at least, I was still alive.

I felt the bed beneath me and sank down into its blissful softness, into darkness. Time no longer had meaning. Past and present merged into one. Was it Celia or Abigail lying in this bed, the darkness gently drifting over her.

I heard Jason's voice. It sounded thin and far away. "Rest now, Abigail."

He called me Abigail, I thought, groping, bewildered, through the darkness and grasping stubbornly at this truth. I was Abigail then, not Celia. And I was alive. I mustn't give up. I had to keep trying.

I heard the bedroom door close, then silence except for the storm, prowling outside the house. Painfully I forced my eyelids open. Each lid felt as heavy as if it were weighted. I sat up, holding onto the great bedposts for support, the room swimming dizzily around me.

I started for the door but the floor dipped beneath me, and I fell to my knees. "Help me!" I cried. "Someone help me."

When the door opened again, I thought at first it was Jason returning and I shrank back. But it was Charlotte who stood in the doorway. She must have been lying down in her room. She was wearing her nightgown and a robe, and her hair was pushed back beneath an old-fashioned mobcap. The hair beneath the cap was a skimpy, unattractive salt and pepper gray. It was a wig, I thought, startled. All that beautiful white, carefully waved and curled hair was a wig, and I felt a childish desire to giggle. But with relief. It was all right now. Charlotte would see that nothing happened to me. Even if Jason returned, he wouldn't dare do anything to me with his sister-in-law there.

"What is it, Abigail? Are you ill?"

She closed the door behind her and started toward me, then stopped, her glance caught by the green velvet gown I had dropped across a chair by the fireplace. She took a deep, startled breath. "Why, that's . . . isn't that Celia's?" Her glance swung to me and her white skin had the yellowed look of old, thin parchment. "Where did you find it?"

"In the attic, in Celia's trunk." My tongue felt thick, swollen in my mouth so it was difficult to speak. "Celia was wearing it when she was killed." And then, as if it were necessary to speak the words aloud, to exorcise them, "When Jason killed her."

A shadow slipped across Charlotte's beautiful, deep set eyes, but she said nothing. I cried accusingly, "You know that, don't you? You've always known."

Charlotte lifted me to my feet, gently helped me back into bed. "I suspected it, yes. That last night when I visited Celia, I saw her traveling gown lying across the bed. I thought it strange, but then we . . . we quarreled. She said terrible things. Even when she had made up her mind to run off with Brian, she couldn't resist tormenting me. The next morning when we found her, I wondered where her traveling gown was, but so many things were happening, the shocking way she had died, Jason's obstinate refusal to talk to anyone, the arrangements for the funeral, there wasn't time to think about a missing gown. Until later. Then I decided it was best not to think about it at all, to accept Jason's explanation that the death was an accident. There was the Barclay name to think about, the disgrace . . ."

"How did Jason find out about Celia's leaving him?"

Charlotte frowned. "I don't know, unless Giles told him. If Rowena did see him return and go into the stable that night, he might have seen something suspicious, perhaps the horses were saddled. He could have gone to Silver Grove and brought Jason back. It was a large party and by that time of night, the gentlemen would have had too much to drink to notice the guest of honor was missing."

Yes, Giles knew, I thought numbly, remembering that gloating look on his face. That was the hold he had over Jason all these years; why Jason could never dismiss the plantation manager no matter his insolence, until I had pushed things too far, insisted that Jason question Giles. Jason must have known he couldn't trust Giles to keep quiet any longer. Not with bribes. It was necessary to silence Giles permanently. And so another accident had been arranged.

I shivered convulsively. My face and body felt encased in ice and yet my gown and hair were soaking wet with perspiration, as if I had a fever.

Charlotte pushed me back among the pillows, her voice solicitous. "You must lie quiet, my dear. You've had a terrible shock. Brandy is what you need. I'll fetch some." I leaned back against the pillows, closing my eyes, wishing I could blot out the look on Jason's face, the fear I had seen there when I had been babbling about finding Celia's gown. He must have known then that I knew what had happened to Celia, that silencing Giles was not enough. I heard Mrs. Barclay returning, felt a glass pressed against my lips. I swallowed too much and the brandy burned my throat. I choked and coughed.

"Drink all of it, Abigail." Charlotte sat down beside the bed. "It'll give you strength. We must plan, you know what is to become of you."

I opened my eyes. "Become of me?" I asked sleepily, taking another swallow of the brandy. It helped to cut through the cottony haze in my mind so that for a moment I could think clearly.

"Well, under the circumstances, you certainly will want to leave Fernwood as soon as possible," she said practically, and then, her voice uncomfortable. "It might not even be . . . safe, if you stayed."

"Jason . . . wouldn't . . ." My voice faltered, died. Because wasn't that why I had tried to run away in the first place, because I was afraid of what Jason might do?

Charlotte shook her head, her face grave. "We don't know, do we? Jason has kept his secret all these years. If you had married him, he might have felt safe, but now, well, it's a chance you mustn't take."

"What can I do?" The effect of the brandy was wearing off. Thoughts slipped through my mind, slippery as silk. I couldn't grasp them for long.

Charlotte frowned at the window, at the rain beginning to beat at the panes. "With this storm, you won't be able to leave tonight. What I suggest is that you get a good night's sleep with your doors bolted and locked on the inside. The first thing in the morning, before anyone's awake, I'll have Jonas drive you to Crossroads. There's a coach that will take you to the station at Leestown in time to catch the nine o'clock train for Richmond. You'll be safe there."

I let my eyes close, drowsily content to allow someone else to make the decisions, take the load off my shoulders. Jason's face swam before me, not the way he had looked in the stable, but filled with tenderness as it was that morning in the rose garden, when all barriers between us had been struck down. The gentle teasing humor in his smile . . . no, I thought bewildered, that wasn't Jason's face, that was Brian's. How like and yet unlike the two brothers, one a murderer, one a fugitive . . .

My eyes flew open. I reached for Mrs. Barclay's hand. "Brian?" I whispered. "What happened to Brian?"

Had he just stood by and watched the woman he loved shot down before his eyes? Then ridden away from Fernwood without a word of protest, taken on his brother's guilt as his own. No man, not even Brian, could be that unselfish, that noble.

Mrs. Charlotte's hand felt curiously limp in mine, as if it were flesh without bones. "Brian left Fernwood that night," she said. "I saw him leave." There was an odd, stiff quality in her voice, as if she were speaking by rote. But just for a moment, she had leaned forward into the lamplight and I saw her eyes clearly for the first time. They stabbed through me, as hostile and vicious as whetted knives.

"You could have been mistaken," I said slowly. "You saw a man on horseback. It could have been Jason returning to the party or Giles."

Too many questions crowded my mind now, jostling, demanding attention. And I was too tired to seek the answers. How strange I should feel so sleepy in the middle of the day, I thought bewildered, the odd, relaxed heaviness in my limbs, the same way I had felt after I took the medicine the doctor had given me, the same sensation of momentary excitement and then the drowsiness pulling me under.

My eyelids jerked open; the shock of my discovery forced me to sit up then sway on my feet beside the bed. "The laudanum!" I thought I screamed the word but my voice came out a thin, reedy whisper. A crash of thunder struck the house broadside; lightning danced at the windows, filling the bedroom with jagged, brilliant light. Charlotte turned, startled, looked away from me.

I remembered where the laudanum was kept, in the small rosewood table. I pulled open the drawer, reached inside. Then stared, panic-stricken, at the brown bottle I held in my hand. The last time I had used the laudanum, it had been almost full. Now it was half empty.

The bottle dropped from my nerveless hand. Charlotte turned toward me, frowning a little. Then she took my arms and pushed me gently back upon the bed, plumped the pillows comfortably behind my head.

Her voice was softly disapproving. "It would have been better if you hadn't found out," she said.

The egg nog, I thought. Jason had brought it to me, laced it with rum, but it was Charlotte who had prepared the drink. Who had had the opportunity to dose it liberally with laudanum.

Charlotte pulled a chair up to the bed; her voice became aggrieved. "I had hoped you'd be . . . asleep by now, before Jason returned from the fields at supper time. You can't imagine how upset I was when he returned early and found you. When he told me he was going to fetch the doctor, I began to worry that perhaps it wasn't going to happen in time, but now with the brandy . . ." She looked smugly at my empty brandy glass and nodded. "I really think you will sleep now, Abigail. That much laudanum . . . I learned during the war, of course, when I nursed the soldiers. One has to be very careful with opium poisoning."

I couldn't take my glance away from the woman, as if mesmerized by the glittering hate in those eyes. "Why?" I whispered. "What harm have I done you?"

She laughed, a brittle sound, splintering like glass around me. "You're the enemy; you're one of them. Isn't that enough? You killed my father, my brothers, burned my home, mutilated my husband. Do you think we'll forget? That any of us will forget . . . ever! And if that wasn't bad enough, the minute you came to Fernwood, it began happening all over again, the way it was with that other vile woman, turning brother against brother. Only worse. You had to start meddling. Giles warned me, you know, that you wouldn't stop poking your nose into Celia's death until you found out the whole truth. Naturally, I couldn't let that happen."

"When . . . when did you talk to Giles?"

Mrs. Charlotte's hands folded complacently in her lap.

"Why, the morning I killed him, of course," she said.

CHAPTER TWENTY

"Giles really was a dreadful man." Charlotte shuddered delicately as if even the memory were distasteful. "I never could understand why my husband kept him on as plantation manager. I thought he was too kindhearted to discharge him. Of course, I know now it wasn't kindness at all. It was blackmail. That filthy, wicked man dared to blackmail my husband."

Beneath the coverlet, I tightened my hands into fists, drove my fingernails deliberately, painfuly into the soft flesh of my palms. Somehow I must keep awake. Somehow hold off that deadly sleep. How long would the laudanum take, I wondered, my mouth shriveled, dry with fear. If I could manage to stay awake until Jason returned . . . if I didn't give in to the drowsiness threatening to pull me down into eternal oblivion . . . if I could keep talking . . .

"Why should . . . Giles blackmail your husband?" I asked Charlotte. "It was Jason who . . ." All at once, understanding in a wave of delirious happiness washed over me so that for a moment I forgot everything else. Not Jason, thank God. It wasn't Jason that Giles had fetched from the party at Silver Grove. It was Guy Barclay.

"You've known . . . all along, you've known it was your husband who killed Celia?" I asked, not really caring any longer, only wanting to keep Charlotte talking, anything to hold my attention and keep me from falling asleep.

"How could I have known?" Her face hardened, anger flickering in the brown eyes like the lightning brightening then darkening the bedroom. "It's because of you I found out. Nothing would have changed if you hadn't come to Fernwood; if you hadn't kept harping on Celia's death, insisting that Jason question Giles. The morning when I went for my ride and ran into Giles at the bridge, he still smelled of cheap whiskey, his face cut from the brawl he had been in the night before. I was disgusted with his behavior and told him so. I warned him that Jason was planning to question him about Celia's death, that he'd be sent away from Fernwood. He laughed at me."

Charlotte's voice bristled with outrage. "He told me I shouldn't be so eager to hear the truth about Celia. If I knew what was good for me, I'd stop your prying any further into that girl's death. He boasted that Jason didn't dare get rid of him. Did we think that after all the years he'd spent at Fernwood, that the Barclays could throw him out like a darky with no more working days left in him."

Agitated, Charlotte rose to her feet and began to pace up and down beside the great canopied bed. I had wanted to keep her talking but now I saw I couldn't have stopped her if I wanted to. The words poured out faster and faster as if she were unable to stop herself.

"I got off my horse with my whip in my hand. I told him he'd better be careful what he said. That the Barclays owed him nothing. He had been well paid for his work. He had no claim on Fernwood or the Barclays. He laughed again. I'll never forget how he laughed, all those disgusting yellow teeth. Then he said: He had a claim on one Barclay . . . Quentin. A man has a claim on his own son!"

I must have gasped. I know I felt a whiplash of shock that drove the numbing drowsiness from my mind.

Charlotte turned and stared at me, her eyes narrowing. "So you didn't know everything, did you? No matter. With that inquisitive brain of yours, you would have eventually wormed out the truth. And I couldn't take that chance, you see. I couldn't risk anyone knowing. You can understand that. After all, I couldn't lose Quentin, not to a wretch like Giles. Not to anyone. He's mine, as much my son as if I had borne him, as much a Barclay as any of us. But if one person knew the truth, then the whole county would soon know."

She was right, I thought. I hadn't known but already I had started to wonder. Since Guy killed Celia, then why had Brian run away? I would remember the remains of the dueling pistol Si had found, buried beside the gazebo. Two guns fired. Two deaths that April night. Two bodies, Celia's and Brian's. The second gun buried in the little white garden, the first placed in Celia's hand.

Horror twisted in my throat so I could hardly speak. "Guy . . . murdered them both . . . his own brother . . ."

"Brian's death was an accident. Guy would never have killed his brother. As for Celia Rougier . . ." Charlotte's mouth tightened viciously. "No jury in the South would have convicted my husband for killing that woman, once they knew the truth. Giles remembered the name Rougier from the trips he had made to New Orleans. On his last trip before the wedding, he checked into the Rougier family history. It took some bribing but he finally discovered that one of the Rougiers, a Creole planter near Baton Rouge, had had a daughter by his mulatto mistress. When the woman died, the planter sent the girl to a convent in France to be raised. But as soon as Celia was grown, she ran away to Paris, passed herself off as a white woman of impoverished noble birth. Jason met her . . . well, you know the rest. As soon as Giles found out the truth, he rushed back to Fernwood, arriving late at night. He went on to Silver Grove and slipped my husband away from the party unnoticed.

"When they returned to Fernwood, Guy found Celia and Brian both gone from their rooms. Guy took Brian's dueling pistols, the first guns he could lay his hands on, planning to ride after them. But Giles had already trapped the two of them in the stable. Of course, Guy couldn't let Celia live. If word got out that a Barclay had almost married a black woman, the family would never have lived down the disgrace. When Guy fired the pistol, Brian stepped in front of Celia. He was killed instantly. There was nothing Guy could do for his brother. But there was still Celia. With the second dueling pistol, he shot her as she bent over the body of her lover."

I closed my eyes, wishing I could shut out the sound of

Charlotte's voice, the pictures flooding my mind of that scene in the stable, of what had gone before. Celia lying here in this bed, living in this room, this house. What a stroke of triumphant revenge it must have seemed to her, to have her hand sought in marriage by a scion of an illustrious Southern family. And when she came to Fernwood how it must have secretly amused and delighted her to have the other Barclay brothers all competing for her favor, the favor of a black woman. Had Brian known the truth at the end, I wondered. Had Celia told him? I would never know, but whether she had or not, Brian had died, trying to protect the woman he loved.

Suddenly I realized that Charlotte was no longer talking. The quiet in the room was broken only by the distant rumbling of the storm, moving slowly away now, the soft hissing of the lamp as the kerosene burned low. Drowsiness in warm, soothing waves rolled over me. I must open my eyes, I warned myself dreamily, must keep Charlotte talking. I must. When I pried my lids apart, and it was agony to do so, the rays of light from the lamp stung my face like tiny flames burning my skin.

"Was it Giles's idea?" I murmured sleepily. "To make Celia's death seem an accident?"

Charlotte sat down again beside the bed. I think she knew what I was trying to do, but the arrogance with which she resumed talking made me realize how confident she was that nothing would save me, only postpone for a while the inevitable.

"I doubt if my husband was in any condition to do more than return to Silver Grove. It was Giles who must have taken care of the bodies, carried Celia to this bedroom, dressed her in her nightgown, placed the gun in her hand. It was Giles I must have seen riding off on Brian's horse, wearing Brian's coat. And it had to be Giles who for his own reasons later spread the rumor that he had seen Brian alive in New Orleans. He had a woman there and she was carrying his child. Somehow he had conceived the insane idea that he was entitled to his share of Fernwood. He brought his son . . ." The voice faltered a moment . . . "He brought Quentin to Fernwood and threatened Guy if he didn't accept the child as Brian's son, he'd expose the whole story. Guy would have been forgiven for killing Celia, but never for killing his own brother. And the war wasn't that long over then . . . there were still carpetbaggers who might be sitting on the jury, who would happily see a Southerner hang for murder."

For the first time Charlotte's voice trembled. "As for me . . . from the minute they put Quentin in my arms, my husband knew I could never give him up. Giles promised my husband he would never interfere with Quentin's life; that he just wanted to be sure Quentin's right to his inheritance as Brian's son would be in Mr. Barclay's will. And my husband must have promised because Quentin is in his will. Only my husband was too honorable a man. He couldn't keep his promise to Giles. I remember the morning he was killed he told me he was riding into town to meet with Judge Colter, our family lawyer, something to do with changing his will, nothing I need worry about."

"Guy . . . fell . . . an accident . . ." I mumbled, each word pushed from my mouth like a stone.

"It was murder." The bitterness burning in Charlotte's eyes was like a madness, driving her. "All these years I thought Quentin was imagining things when he said he saw the cavalier take a rock and kill my husband. It was true. Giles waited in the road for my husband, then suddenly appeared out of the mist wearing the cavalier's costume. Nothing but an apparition appearing that way could have unseated Guy. He was a superb horseman, even with one arm."

"Giles . . . told you . . ."

"He told me enough. He smiled and said I should be grateful to him. That he had made sure Quentin would never be disinherited. That drunken sot had taken everything from me, my son, my husband, and he was acting as if I should thank him. He was still smiling when I hit him with my whip across the side of his head. It was so unexpected. He stumbled and lost his balance, fell off the bridge into the pond. I watched him go under. I was afraid when they found him, he'd still have that silly, drunken smile on his face."

Before my eyes Charlotte Barclay seemed to shrink in her chair, become an old, ravaged woman, her face drained a bloodless white beneath the wispy gray hair, only her eyes alive, burning with a savage exultation. I thought of these last days since Giles's death, the change in the woman, so gradual no one had noticed except perhaps Dulcy. Charlotte keeping to her room more and more, the nervous way her hands lately were never still where before they had always lain, disciplined, controlled in her lap. The strain she had been living under since Giles's death would have crushed any woman, even one of weaker fiber than Charlotte Barclay.

Almost I could feel pity for her, except I had no strength left for pity. A great weight was settling on my chest, crushing me. It was an impossible effort to simply try and force air in and out of my lungs. I struggled to sit erect, to push the weight away, and the movement of my arms, stirring weakly brought Charlotte closer, so near I could catch the lemon verbena scent she wore, her voice lulling, soothing.

"Sleep now, Abigail. I'll stay here beside you. It's better this way. No one wants you here at Fernwood. And you have no one waiting for you at home, no family, no friends. No one anywhere who cares what happens to you."

"Jason . . . Jason . . ."

"Oh, I don't expect him back for a while," Charlotte's voice was complacent. "He'll have to go all the way into Crossroads for the doctor."

She sighed and shook her head. "Poor Rob. He'll be terribly upset. He was so counting on making a wealthy marriage. It's really all that's left for him, of course. When your landlady asked Rob to deliver to you a letter you had received at the boardinghouse, he couldn't resist opening it. It must have seemed a godsend, the mousy Miss Prentice an heiress. Except Jason, clumsy, stiff-necked Jason, had somehow managed to turn your head first. You must admit it was very clever of Rob, hiding the lawyer's letter in Jason's room, knowing Rowena was sure to find it, sure to tell you. Rowena never could keep a secret."

"No one . . . believe . . . my dying . . ." My tongue was a balloon, filling my mouth. I was shivering again, my body soaked in icy perspiration.

"Oh, I think they will." Charlotte nodded agreeably, smiling gently. "You must admit you have been behaving strangely, my dear. Chasing ghosts and falling into cold cellars. And who can say what a young, distraught woman, crossed in love, might do? An accidental overdose of laudanum, self-administered. After all, what else could it be? Who else was in the house with you, except me, and what possible motive could I have?" Her smile faded a little, disappointed. "It is too bad you didn't tell anyone about the ghost you saw in the drawing room last night, considering all the trouble I went to . . ."

"It was you." I no longer had the strength to speak but she could read the accusation in my eyes.

She nodded, pleased. "Perhaps I wasn't as effective as Giles was in the garden, but the hidden room made it all very easy. All I had to do was wait until Jason went upstairs." Her voice grew thoughtful. "It's strange, you know, but at first I almost believed you did see the cavalier in the garden that night. There have been times when I thought . . ." She shrugged. "Well, I suppose we all have our fancies. And now, my dear, I really do think we've talked enough. You must be very sleepy. I'll just sit quietly here beside you." Her gaze roamed around the room, as if wanting to make sure that everything was in order. All at once, she got to her feet, frowning. "Now where is that laudanum bottle?" she murmured annoyed. "It should be found on the table beside you."

Vaguely, I remembered the bottle dropping from my hand. Charlotte must have remembered, too, for she dropped to her knees, peered exasperated under the bed. I couldn't see her but I could hear her edging further beneath the bed. The bottle must have rolled out of reach . . .

Now, I thought. My eyes fastened on the door to the sitting room. If I could reach the veranda and down the back stairs, I could hide in the overgrown jungle of the garden, stay hidden, until Jason returned with the doctor.

Jason. I moaned without sound. No matter how feeble, I had to make an effort to survive. Despite what Charlotte thought, I would not willingly drift off into death; I would not leave Jason while I could still breathe, still nurse even a faint instinct to live. Gathering my strength into one last concentrated effort, I struggled from the bed, clinging to the bedpost as the floor dipped crazily beneath my feet.

I could hear Charlotte rummaging under the bed, muttering irritably at the elusive bottle. I dragged myself across the room, lurching from chair to table, to fireplace, to the door at last, my feet soundless on the rug.

Then I was through the sitting room, my hand on the latch that opened the door onto the veranda. The wind caught the door and I practically fell forward onto the veranda. Splinters of wood drove into my knees, the rain stinging my face like pellets.

I crawled to the balustrade, clung to it for support, began to inch my way along its length toward the staircase. Overhead the clouds were still a yellowish gray, the garden dark and shadowy below me, the rain soaking me to the skin before I had taken two steps. But at least the rain revived me a little, helped me fight off the deadly weariness that made me feel as if I had sad irons attached to each ankle, a colossal effort of will merely to lift one foot after the other.

Then I felt hands dig into my shoulder, pull me around roughly. Charlotte's arms were like wire tightening around me, her face livid with rage. How strong she is, I thought, almost absently . . . all those years of horseback riding. She pulled my hands free from the railing as easily as if I were a child. All strength left me. My body collapsed, a dead weight against her. She shifted her arms to take a firmer grip, then I felt her body stiffen.

Her gaze was no longer on me. Her eyes stared beyond me down into the garden. I saw her face. There was no anger there now, only a shocked terror. Bewildered I followed her gaze. A dark figure had appeared in the garden beneath us, a shadow detaching itself from the shadows, a caped figure moving toward the house. Just for a second, the pincher grip loosened on my shoulders. I fell to my knees.

I heard a sound come from Charlotte's throat, a whistling, disbelieving intake of breath. She stepped closer to the balustrade, to take a closer look. I recognized before Charlotte did the sound of the balustrade creaking, protesting at her weight leaning against it. I remembered the treachery of that balustrade. I tried to cry out a warning, but no sound came from my swollen mouth. No sound came even when I heard the wood crack and saw the sudden awareness, too late, flood Charlotte's face.

Her arms thrust out to catch at something, anything, to regain her balance. One hand lightly brushed my hair as she pitched forward, disappeared from my view. She cried out once. I felt the thud beneath me as her body struck the flagstone terrace, but still I could make no sound. I crouched, trembling, on all fours, my body shaking. I could not speak even when Jason, wrapped in a cape, bent over me, his face shocked, "Abigail, are you all right? For God's sake, what's happened?"

The last thing I remembered, Jason's voice calling to me, before the darkness that would no longer be held back, swept triumphantly over me, pulling me under.

CHAPTER TWENTY-ONE

At first, I was left alone in the darkness. Then someone was shaking me, shouting at me, pouring a nasty tasting liquid down my throat. My stomach muscles contracted and I was violently sick. Arms pulled me erect, forced me to walk back and forth, back and forth, an endless, futile treadmill to nowhere. Whenever I stumbled, started to collapse with weariness, something cold and wet flicked painfully across my face. I cried out indignantly at the outrage to no avail. I wanted to demand why I was being so cruelly treated, I tried to call out for Jason, but all my strength was concentrated in my legs, being relentlessly propelled forward, stumbling, falling, ruthlessly thrust forward again.

The only time I was allowed to rest was when coffee, hot and bitter, was forced to my lips, spilling from my mouth down my gown when I could swallow no more. Then the arms once more pulled me to my feet, the walking began all over again. Dimly I began to realize first it was Jason beside me, then Dr. Marshall, always begging, ordering, cajoling me to walk, refusing to allow me to stop no matter how I pleaded with them to leave me in peace, to let me sleep.

Finally, was it hours, days later, I would never know . . . every nerve and muscle in my body screamed with exhaustion . . . I was aware of sun coming in the windows, a glaring morning sun, and a voice saying, "Let her sleep now. There's nothing more we can do."

Sleep, when it came, was not peaceful. It was filled with nightmares, monstrous demons pursuing me, hot flames licking at me, then bitter, freezing cold. I fled down endless halls but no matter how fast I ran, I could sense the fetid breath of my pursuer, close on my heels.

When finally my nightmares forced me awake, I saw that I was again in the canopied bed. The shades were drawn and a lamp burned dimly. I could barely make out the figure of a woman slumped in a chair beside the bed. For one horror-filled moment, I thought it was Charlotte Barclay returned to keep her death vigil and I cried aloud.

At the sound, Rowena awoke instantly and came to stand beside the bed. She looked thinner, if possible, more gaunt. "How are you feeling?" she asked.

"Better. How long have you . . ." I groped for memory. "Have I been ill long?"

"It's almost a week now, first from the effects of an overdose of laudanum, then a fever set in. It's a miracle Dr. Marshall pulled you through."

As she briskly presented the facts, memory returned, a curtain lifting. Charlotte and I struggling on the veranda, the caped figure coming through the garden, the sound of the balustrade groaning, giving way beneath Charlotte, her hand brushing, almost caressing, my hair as she fell away from me. And that last final sound I knew I would never forget.

I swallowed; my throat felt parched. "Mrs. Barclay . . . is she . . ."

Even before Rowena spoke, I knew what the answer would be. "Aunt Charlotte never recovered consciousness." Then, her shrill voice, shaking, "I told and told Jason that that balustrade was filled with dry rot!"

I leaned back weakly, turned my face away. So it was ended. Despite what Charlotte had feared, I would never have given away her secret if she had lived. I had no intention of betraying her now that she was dead.

Rowena brought me some hot broth and after I finished it, I felt stronger. I wanted to ask Rowena where Jason was, but the pewter eyes were already filling with questions. Since I had no wish to answer them, I closed my eyes and pretended to sleep.

The next few days I was content to eat whatever Rowena

brought me and slip in and out of sleep. No one visited me except Rowena and the doctor although once I awakened at night and thought I saw Jason standing beside the bed, but when I awoke in the morning I was alone and knew I had dreamed it. My eyes burned with unshed tears of disappointment. That was ended, too. There was no way I could tell Jason the truth without involving Charlotte and Quentin. Remembering how I had fought against Jason in the stable, the horror and fear he must have seen in my face, I wondered if I could find the courage to face him again, even to say my goodbyes.

The fourth day I convinced the doctor that I was well enough to sit up. Dulcy came to help me into my robe, settled me in the large wing chair by the fireplace, her hands gentle but her eyes mourning. Then in the other wing chair across from me, almost hidden in the shadows, I saw Celia's traveling dress, still left where I had dropped it. Dulcy saw it, too, and frowning at the oversight, picked it up hastily.

"It's all right, Dulcy," I said. I had made my peace with Celia days before. The sight of her gown didn't upset me. I looked up at the woman, fumbled for words. "I'm sorry . . . about . . . if I could only have reached her in time."

"No, ma'am." Dulcy's voice was quiet, as if she at least understood and I had no need to explain. "What happened to Mrs. Charlotte, happened a long time ago, during the war when she saw her house burn and her father killed. She was always soft and sweet but afterwards, she changed. Lots of white folks did after the war. Like something had twisted inside them, only from the outside, you couldn't tell."

"How is Quentin?"

"Oh, he's grievin' for Mrs. Charlotte, but it'll pass." Dulcy shrugged philosophically. "Young folks, troubles run like water off a duck's back."

After she had left, I sighed and settled back in the chair, drawing an afghan up over my knees. Dulcy might understand but sooner or later I would have to start giving explanations to Jason, think of some lies to cover up what had really happened. I suppose I could convince him that I had accidentally taken an overdose of laudanum but how could I explain away what he had seen with his own eyes on the veranda, my struggling with Mrs. Barclay like a mad woman.

I was so intent on my own thoughts that I didn't hear the door open until Jason cleared his throat and I looked up startled to see him standing, hesitantly, in the doorway. "I didn't knock because I thought you might be asleep and I didn't want to disturb you." He paused, uncertain, his face ill at ease. "How are you feeling?"

"Much better, thank you." We might have been two strangers, exchanging pleasantries.

He came into the room, stopped before the fireplace. "I would have been here sooner but I was afraid my presence might upset . . ." He broke off and I dropped my gaze, embarrassed, knowing we were both remembering those moments in the stable.

Jason began again. "The doctor says you'll be able to travel in a few days. No doubt, after everything's that happened, you're anxious to leave. I've talked to Rob. He'll be happy to accompany you to Boston."

"That isn't necessary." I had forgotten all about Rob, about the letter from my attorneys he had deliberately hidden in Jason's room, to turn me against Jason. But not just Rob's fault, I thought, mine, too, for not trusting Jason enough, for not having enough confidence in myself, as a woman.

Suddenly Jason's hand tightened into a fist and he struck at the mantelpiece so the delicate gold candlesticks jumped. "If only I hadn't been such a jealous idiot," he exploded. "If I hadn't kept you here when you wanted to leave, you would have been spared all this." His face darkened, looking down at me. "When I think of how close Charlotte came to killing you . . ."

The shock I felt was like coming from a dark cave into blinding sunlight. I leaned forward, the afghan falling from my lap, unheeded. "You know? But how? Rowena said Charlotte died without regaining consciousness."

"She never fully regained her senses, but there were a few minutes, when Rowena was here nursing you. I was sitting with

Charlotte. She was delirious. She said things about Brian and Celia . . . and Guy. Not much but enough to start me thinking." He pulled up a chair, brought it directly before me and sat down so I had to meet his gaze. His voice was quiet. "I think now, Abigail, if you're feeling strong enough, you'd better tell me the rest."

And so I told him, at least, part of it, my suspicions about Celia's death, my visit to the attic and what I had finally learned from Mrs. Barclay, about the double murder. Jason listened, without interrupting, his face dark and sober. Yet I had the feeling that he wasn't really surprised at what I was telling him.

When I finished, he nodded. "We found Celia's bloodstained traveling gown. Rowena recognized it. I think I guessed the truth then. Rob told me about the pistol you found in the garden and we searched Giles's effects. We found this, tucked away in a drawer." He held out to me a man's old-fashioned gold pocket watch. "It belonged to Brian. The watch disappeared the same night he did. Everyone thought he had taken it with him. Giles must have removed the watch from Brian's body before he buried him. Maybe he thought it was too valuable to bury, or perhaps he was keeping it as proof later if Guy balked at his blackmail."

"Buried him?" I fought a sick feeling of horror. "You found Brian's body?"

"Only a few feet beneath the spot in the garden where you and Si found the dueling pistol. I remembered that the trenches had been dug in the garden the day before the wedding, ready for the plants Guy had ordered for the garden. It must have seemed the handiest place for Giles to dispose of the body. It had to be Giles," he said grimly. "Guy would never have had the stomach for it. Any more than he could continue to live under the threat of Giles's blackmail, let alone allow another man to be blamed for his guilt. Giles underestimated Guy. I'm not saying my brother was a strong man but he had his own code of honor."

"Guy's death wasn't an accident," I said. "Quentin wasn't imagining things when he saw the cavalier strike down his uncle." I had to be sure that that cloud, at least, was lifted from

Quentin's young shoulders. "The boy did see murder committed."

Jason shook his head wearily. "I can understand why Giles felt he had to get rid of Guy before he changed his will, to protect his son's inheritance, but what I don't understand is why Guy killed Celia and Brian in the first place. All I could make out from Charlotte's ravings was that Guy had killed Celia . . . that Celia was black, evil. I always knew she hated Celia. But Guy? Why should he harm Celia?"

When I did not answer at once, he lifted my chin and forced me to look at him. "I want to hear all of it, Abigail," he said gravely.

So I told him the part I had deliberately left out, about Giles's discovery in New Orleans of Celia's ancestry. When I finished, he walked over to the window, stood with his back to me for a long moment. When he spoke, his voice was bitter. "I'd like to tell myself it wouldn't have made any difference to me, if I had known. But, of course, that's a lie. Yet I can remember loving her so much that when she looked at another man, I felt as if I were tearing apart inside. Even though I sensed, no matter how close we were, that there was a part of her I couldn't possess completely, that always eluded me. I thought it was my fault, some lack in me. That last night when she told me she had changed her mind about the marriage, I must have gone crazy. I tried to force her to love me, clumsily, stupidly, tried to prove to her that I was as much a man as Brian.

"I couldn't go through with it. So instead I tried to destroy her with words. I laughed at her. I told her that if she thought Brian would marry her, that she was deluding herself. That Brian was only amusing himself with her, that he wasn't the marrying sort. Later, I was sure it was what I had done to her, what I said to her that night that drove her to suicide."

Jason turned to face me, his shoulders held stiffly, his eyes holding a bleached anguish. He shrugged helplessly. "Now I wonder. Perhaps I was wrong. Perhaps finally Brian had found a woman he could love. At least, I'm thankful that at the end they were together."

I couldn't bear to see him tearing open old wounds that should have been healed long ago. "What of Quentin?" I asked quickly. "Have you told him?"

"No, he's too young now. Later, when he's older, I'll tell him the truth. Or as much of it as he needs to know. And I intend to see that he has an inheritance of his own. I suppose the truth is I've always felt guilty about Quentin. I've never been able to feel close to the boy. He reminded me too much of what I wanted to forget. I knew Charlotte was smothering the boy, that it wasn't healthy . . ."

An undercurrent of anger ran beneath Jason's voice when he spoke of his sister-in-law. "She must have been mad, first Giles, then you."

"I don't believe Charlotte meant to kill Giles," I said slowly. "It was an accident."

"The same kind of accident that would have killed you," Jason said roughly. "If I hadn't run into Dr. Marshall on my way into town, we would never have reached Fernwood in time to save you. Or if Charlotte had known more about how laudanum works."

At my puzzled look, he explained. "Remember I put rum into the egg nog that Charlotte had already spiked with the laudanum? When that didn't work fast enough, she put the drug in the brandy she gave you. Dr. Marshall tells me that taking liquor along with laudanum slows down the effect of the drug. Otherwise, he says, you could never have fought off the laudanum as long as you did."

I didn't want to remember those moments, though, when I had struggled to stay awake, to stay alive. And I asked instead, "One thing still bothers me. The cape you wore when you came across the garden, Jason. I've never seen you wear one before."

He looked bewildered at my question then his face cleared. "Oh, that cape. It isn't mine. When I left you here in the house, I rushed off without any coat. On my way back with the doctor, it started to rain. At the stable, I grabbed the first covering I saw to throw around me. It happened to be Giles's old Inverness cape he always kept hanging by the door. Why? What difference does it make?"

"No difference," I said. No difference to anyone except Charlotte and me. For I had seen the look on her face when she glimpsed the caped figure crossing the garden. For one frightening moment she had believed it was the cavalier, coming to claim his next victim. And it was that one moment that had saved me.

Jason knelt to replace the afghan that had slipped to the floor. As he tucked it around me, his hand brushed mine. He looked as if he were about to speak, then hesitated and started to draw his hand away. My throat tightened. There had been so much left unspoken between us already. Both of us too proud to show our true feelings. Too wary of being hurt, fearful of being betrayed again. We could only begin once more if all that was finished for good. Whether I swallowed my pride and made the first move, or Jason, what difference did it make?

My hand reached out, fastened firmly around his. "Jason," I said quietly. "Don't send me away. Let me stay."

Startled, his glance met mine, and then there was no holding back for either of us. The next thing I knew he pulled me to my feet and we were clinging together, as if we could not get close enough to each other. Not kissing but simply holding on to each other as if for dear life.

Rowena bustled into the room, saw us in the embrace and stammered, "I'm . . . sorry. I . . . I thought you might need something." Then she turned and fled.

Jason cocked an amused eyebrow. "I'm afraid we've shocked Cousin Rowena."

I remembered the red-faced, lanky man I had seen in the kitchen with Rowena. Perhaps in time without her aunt to influence Rowena against him . . .

"It might be nice, after we're married, if we invite Mr. Watkins to dinner," I said thoughtfully.

"Sam! He'd never come."

"Oh, I think he would," I said demurely. "If you asked him."

Jason gave me a quizzical glance, then suddenly laughed,

deep in his throat. His laughter filled the blue room, drove the last of the dark shadows from the corners, dissolving them in the sunlight spilling through the open windows. The musty odor had completely disappeared. The air smelled fresh and sweet. So sweet that for a moment I thought I caught a light scent of roses, heady, indescribably fragrant. Or was it only the perfume from Celia's green velvet gown still lingering in the air. I don't suppose I'll ever know.

For the next moment Jason's arms tightened around me, his lips reached for mine. And a breeze rustled the curtains, softly as a sigh, and bore the fragrance away.